"What If I Say No?"

Not an option. Conrad played his trump card. "Do you want my signature on those divorce papers?"

Jayne dropped her rings on top of the computer that just happened to be resting over the divorce papers. "Are you blackmailing me?"

"Call it a trade." He rested his hand over the five-carat diamond he'd chosen for her, only her. "You give me two days and I'll give you the divorce papers. Signed."

"Just two days?" She studied him through narrowed, suspicious eyes.

He gathered up the rings and pressed them to her palm, closing her fingers over them again. "Forty-eight hours."

Forty-eight hours to romance her back into his bed one last time.

Dear Reader,

For as long as I can remember, I have adored James Bond movies—the glitz, the glamour, the thrills! Regardless of the actor, 007's alpha appeal has certainly stood the test of time. Some of my favorite Bond movies include Monte Carlo-based *Casino Royale, Never Say Never Again* and *GoldenEye*. (Dreamy sigh!)

However, beyond the glitz, glamour and thrills, the part of the Bond mystique that touched my heart most came from seeing such an indomitable hero fall truly and deeply in love, like in *On Her Majesty's Secret Service*. What a treat to write a story about my own Monte Carlo secret-agent hero as he secures happily ever after with his one true love!

Thank you for choosing an Alpha Brotherhood read. I'm pleased to say there will be more in the series, the next one featuring Malcolm Douglas in *Playing for Keeps*.

Happy reading!

Cheers,

Cathy

http://catherinemann.com
Facebook: facebook.com/CatherineMannAuthor
Twitter: @CatherineMann1

All or Nothing

CATHERINE MANN

MILLS & BOON®

First published in Great Britain 2013
by Mills & Boon, an imprint of Harlequin (UK) Limited.
Large Print edition 2013
Harlequin (UK) Limited,
Eton House, 18-24 Paradise Road,
Richmond, Surrey TW9 1SR

© Catherine Mann 2013

ISBN: 978 0 263 23785 6

Harlequin (UK) policy is to use papers that are natural, renewable and recyclable products and made from wood grown in sustainable forests. The logging and manufacturing process conform to the legal environmental regulations of the country of origin.

Printed and bound in Great Britain
by CPI Antony Rowe, Chippenham, Wiltshire

CATHERINE MANN

USA TODAY bestselling author Catherine Mann lives on a sunny Florida beach with her flyboy husband and their four children. With more than forty books in print in over twenty countries, she has also celebrated wins for both a RITA® Award and a Booksellers' Best Award. Catherine enjoys chatting with readers online—thanks to the wonders of the internet, which allows her to network with her laptop by the water! Contact Catherine through her website, www.catherinemann.com, find her on Facebook and Twitter (@CatherineMann1) or reach her by snail mail at PO Box 6065, Navarre, FL 32566, USA.

To Shelley, welcome to the family!
Love you much!

One

Monte Carlo, Casino de la Méditerranée

It wasn't every day that a woman bet her five-carat, yellow-diamond engagement ring at a roulette table. But it was the only way Jayne Hughes could think of to get her pigheaded husband to take the rock back.

She'd left Conrad messages, telling him to contact her attorney. Conrad ignored them. Her lawyer had called his, to no avail. Divorce papers had been couriered, hand delivered to Conrad's personal secretary, who'd been told not to sign for them under any circumstances.

As Jayne angled through the crush of gamblers toward the roulette table, her fist closed around the engagement ring Conrad had given her seven years ago. Since he owned the *Casino de la Méditerranée,* if she lost the long-shot bet, the ring would be back in his possession. All or nothing, she had to lose to win. She just wanted a clean break and no more heartache.

Jayne plunked down the ring on the velvet square for 12 red. The anniversary of their breakup fell on January 12, next week. They'd spent three years of their seven years married apart. By now Conrad should have been able to accept that so they could move on with their lives.

Familiar sounds echoed up the domed ceiling, chimes and laughter, squeals of excitement mixed with the "ahhhh" of defeat. She'd called these walls full of frescoes home for the four years they'd lived together as man and wife. Even though she moved with ease here now, she'd grown up in a more down-to-earth home in Miami. Her father's dental practice had kept them very comfortable. Of course, they would have been a lot more comfortable had her father not been hiding away a second family.

Regardless, her parents' finances were nowhere close to touching the affluence of this social realm.

Her ring had been a Van Cleef & Arpels, one-of-a-kind design that had dazzled her back when she believed in fairy tales.

Cinderella had left the building. Jayne's glass slipper had been shattered right along with her heart. Prince Charming didn't exist. She made her own destiny and would take charge of her own life.

Nodding to the croupier in charge of spinning the wheel, she nudged her ring forward, centering it on the number 12 red. The casino employee tugged his tie and frowned, looking just past her shoulders and giving her only a second's warning before…

Conrad.

She could feel his presence behind her without looking. And how damn unfair was that? Even after three years apart, never once laying eyes on him the entire time, her body still knew him. Wanted him. Her skin tingled under the silky beige gown and her mind filled with memories of spending an entire weekend making love with the Mediterranean breeze blowing in through the balcony doors.

Conrad's breath caressed her ear an instant ahead of his voice. "Gaming plaques can be obtained to your left, *mon amour*."

My love.

Hardly. More like his possession. "And divorce papers can be picked up from my lawyer."

She was a hospice nurse. Not a freaking princess.

"Now why would I want to split up when you look hot enough to melt a man's soul?" A subtle shift of his feet brought him closer until his fire seared her back as tangibly as the desire—and anger—pumping through her veins.

She pivoted to face him, bracing for the impact of his good looks.

Simply seeing him sent her stomach into a

predictable tumble. She resented the way her body reacted to him. Why, why, why couldn't her mind and her hormones synch up?

His jet-black hair gleamed under the massive crystal chandeliers and she remembered the thick texture well, surprisingly soft and totally luxurious. She'd spent many nights watching him sleep and stroking her fingers along his hair. With his eyes closed, the power of his espresso-brown gaze couldn't persuade her to go against her better judgment. He didn't sleep much, an insomniac, as if he couldn't surrender control to the world even for sleep. So she'd cherished those rare, unguarded moments to look at him.

Women stared and whispered whenever Conrad Hughes walked past. Even now they didn't try to hide open stares of appreciation. He was beyond handsome in his tuxedo—or just wearing jeans and a T-shirt—in a bold and brooding way. While one hundred percent an American from New York, he had the exotic look of some Italian or Russian aristocrat from another century.

He was also chock-full of arrogance.

Conrad scooped the five-carat diamond off the velvet, and she only had a second to celebrate her victory before he placed it in her palm, closing her fingers back over the ring. The cool stone warmed with his hand curling hers into a fist.

"Conrad," she snapped, tugging.

"Jayne," he rumbled right back, still clasping until the ring cut into her skin. Shifting, he tucked alongside her. "This is hardly the place for our reunion."

He started walking and since he still held her hand, she had no choice but to go along, past the murmuring patrons and thick carved pillars. Familiar faces broke up the mass of vacationers, but she couldn't pause to make idle chitchat, pretending to be happy around old friends and employees.

Her husband's casino provided a gathering place for the elite, even royalty. At last count, he owned a half dozen around the world, but the *Casino de la Méditerranée* had always been his favorite, as well as his primary residence. The old-world flair included antique machines and tables, even though their internal mechanisms were upgraded to state of the art.

People vacationed here to cling to tradition, dressed to the nines in Savile Row tuxedos and Christian Dior evening gowns. Diamonds and other jewels glittered, no doubt original settings from Cartier to Bvlgari. Her five-carat ring was impressive, no question, but nothing out of the ordinary at the *Casino de la Méditerranée.*

Her high heels clicked faster and faster against the marble tiles, her black metallic bag slipping down to her elbow in her haste. "Stop. It. Now."

"No. Thanks." He stopped in front of the gilded elevator, his private elevator, and thumbed the button.

"God, you're still such a sarcastic ass." She sighed under her breath.

"Well, damn." He hooked an arm around her shoulders. "I've never heard that before. Thanks for enlightening me. I'll take it under advisement."

Jayne shrugged off his arm and planted her heels. "I am not going up to your suite."

"Our penthouse apartment." He plucked the ring from her hand and dropped it into her black bag hanging from her shoulder. "Our home."

A home? Hardly. But she refused to argue with him here in the lobby where anyone could listen. "Fine, I need to talk to you. Alone."

The doors slid open. He waived the elevator attendant away and led her inside, sealing them in the mirrored cubicle. "Serving the papers won't make me sign them."

So she'd noticed, to her intense frustration. "You can't really intend to stay married and live apart forever."

"Maybe I just wanted you to have the guts to talk to me in person rather than through another emissary—" his deep brown eyes crinkled at the corners "—to tell me to my face that you're prepared to spend the rest of your life never again sharing the same bed."

Sharing a bed again?

Not a chance.

She couldn't trust him, and after what happened with her father? She refused to let any man fool her the way her mother had been duped—or to break her heart the way her mother had been heartbroken. "You mean sharing the same bed whenever you happen to be in town after disappearing for weeks on end. We've been over this a million times. I can't sleep with a man who keeps secrets."

He stopped the elevator with a quick jab and faced her, the first signs of frustration stealing the smile from him. "I've never lied to you."

"No. You just walk away when you don't want to answer the question."

He was a smart man. Too smart. He played with words as adeptly as he played with money. At only fifteen years old, he'd used his vast trust fund to manipulate the stock market. He'd put more than one crook out of business with short sales, and nearly landed himself in a juvenile detention center. His family's influence worked the system. He'd been sentenced by a judge to attend a military reform school instead, where he hadn't reformed in the least, only fine-tuned his ability to get his way.

God help her, she still wasn't immune to him, a large part of why she'd kept her distance and tried to instigate the divorce from overseas. The last straw in their relationship had come when she'd had a scare with a questionable mammogram. She'd desperately needed his support, but couldn't locate him for nearly a week, the longest seven days of her life.

Her health concerns turned out to be benign, but her fears for her marriage? One hundred percent malignant. Out of respect for what they'd shared, she'd waited for Conrad to come home. She'd given him one last chance to be honest with her. He'd fed her the same old tired line about conducting business and how she should trust him.

She'd walked out that night with only a carry-on piece of luggage. If only she'd thought to leave her rings behind then.

Standing here in the intimate confines of the elevator, with classical music piping through the sound system, she could only think of the time he'd pressed her to the mirrored wall and made love to her until she could barely think, much less remember to ask him where he'd been for the past two weeks.

And still he wasn't talking, damn him. "Well, Conrad? You don't have anything to say?"

"The real problem here is not me. It's that you don't know how to trust." He skimmed his finger along the chain strap of her black metallic shoulder bag and hitched it back in place. "I am not your father."

His words turned residual passion into anger— and pain. "That's a low blow."

"Am I wrong?"

He stood an inch away, so close they could lose themselves in a kiss instead of the ache of all this self-awareness. But she couldn't travel that path again. She stepped closer, drawn by the scent of him, the deep ache in her belly to have his lips on hers. The draw was so intense it took everything inside her to step back.

"If you're so committed to the truth, then how about proving *you're* not *your* father."

When Conrad had been arrested as a teen, the

papers ran headlines, Like Father, Like Son. His embezzling dad had escaped conviction as well for his white-collar crimes thanks to that same high-priced lawyer.

In her heart she knew her husband wasn't like his old man. Conrad had hacked into all those Wall Street companies to expose his father and others like him. She knew intellectually…but the evasiveness, the walls between them… She just couldn't live that way.

She reached into her large, dangling evening bag and pulled out the folded stack of papers. "Here. I'm saving you a trip to the lawyer's office."

She pushed them against Conrad's chest and hit the elevator button for her floor, a guest suite, because she couldn't stomach the notion of staying in their old quarters, which she'd once decorated with hope and love.

"Conrad, consider yourself officially served. Don't worry about the ring. I'll sell it and donate the money to charity. All I need from you is your signature."

The elevator doors slid open at her floor, not his, not their old penthouse, but a room she'd prearranged under a different name. Her head held high, she charged out and into the carpeted corridor.

She walked away from Conrad, almost managing to ignore the fact that he still had the power to break her heart all over again.

Conrad had made ten fortunes by thirty-two years old and had given away nine. But tonight, he'd finally hit the jackpot with his biggest win in three years. He had a chance for closure with Jayne so she wouldn't haunt his dreams every damn night for the rest of his life.

He stalked back into the lobby toward the casino to turn over control for the evening. Once he'd been alerted to Jayne's presence on the floor, he'd walked out on a Fortune 500 guest and a deposed royal heir, drawn by the gleam of his wife's light blond hair piled on top of her head, the familiar curve of her pale neck. Talking to Jayne had been his number-one priority.

Finding her thunking down her ring on 12 red hadn't been the highlight of his life, but the way she'd leaned into him, the flare of awareness in her sky-blue eyes? No, it wasn't over, in spite of the divorce papers she'd slapped against his chest.

She was back under his roof for tonight. He folded the papers again and slid them inside his tuxedo jacket. As he walked past the bar, the bartender nodded toward the last brass stool— and a familiar patron.

Damn it. He did not need this now. But there was no dodging Colonel John Salvatore, his former headmaster and current contact for his freelance work with Interpol, work that had pulled him away from Jayne, work that he preferred she not know about for her own safety. Conrad's wealthy lifestyle and influence gave him easy entrée into powerful circles. When Interpol needed an "in" they called on a select group of contract operatives, headed by John Salvatore, saving months creating an undercover persona for a regular agent. Salvatore usually only tapped into his services once or twice a year. If he used Conrad too often, he risked exposure of the whole setup.

The reason for the missing weeks that always had Jayne in such an uproar.

Part of him understood he should just tell her about his second "career." He'd been cleared to share the basics with his spouse, just not details. But another part of him wanted her to trust him, to believe in him rather than assume he was like his criminal father or a cheating bastard like her dad.

The colonel lifted his Scotch in toast. "Someone's in over his head."

Conrad sat on the bar stool next to the colonel in the private corner, not even bothering to deny Salvatore's implication. "Jayne could have seen you there."

And if the colonel was here, there had to be a work reason. The past three years in particular, Conrad had embraced the sporadic missions with Interpol to fill his empty life, but not now.

"Then she would think your old headmaster

came to say hello since I'd already come to see another former student's concert at the Côte d'Azur." Salvatore wore his standard gray suit, red tie and total calm like a uniform.

"This is not a good time." Having Jayne show up unannounced had turned his world upside down.

"I'm just hand delivering some cleanup paperwork—" he passed over a disc, no doubt encrypted "—from our recent…endeavor."

Endeavor: aka the Zhutov counterfeit currency case, which had concluded a month ago.

If Conrad had been thinking with his brain instead of his Johnson, he would have realized the colonel would never risk bringing him into another operation this soon. Already, Jayne was messing with his head, and she hadn't even been back in his life for an hour.

"Everybody wants to give me documents today." He patted the tux jacket and the papers crackled a reminder that his marriage was a signature away from being over.

"You're a popular gentleman tonight."

"I'm sarcastic and arrogant." According to Jayne anyway, and Jayne was a smart woman.

"And incredibly self-aware." Colonel Salvatore finished off his drink, his intense eyes always scanning the room. "You always were, even at the academy. Most of the boys arrived in denial or with delusions about their own importance. You knew your strengths right from the start."

Thinking about those teenage years made Conrad uncomfortable, itchy, reminding him of the toxic time in his life when his father had toppled far and hard off the pedestal Conrad had placed him upon. "Are we reminiscing for the hell of it, sir, or is there a point here?"

"You knew your strengths, but you didn't know your weakness." He nudged aside the cut crystal glass and stood. "Jayne is your Achilles' heel, and you need to recognize that or you're going to self-destruct."

"I'll take that under advisement." The bitter truth of the whole Achilles' heel notion stung like hell since he'd told his buddy Troy much the same thing when the guy had fallen head over ass in love.

"You're definitely as stubborn as ever." Salvatore clapped Conrad on the shoulder. "I'll be in town for the weekend. So let's say we meet again for lunch, day after tomorrow, to wrap up Zhutov. Good night, Conrad."

The colonel tossed down a tip on the bar and tucked into the crowd, blending in, out of sight before Conrad could finish processing what the old guy had said. Although Salvatore was rarely wrong, and he'd been right about Jayne's effect.

But as far as having a *good* night?

A *good* night was highly unlikely. But he had hopes. Because the evening wasn't over by a long shot—as Jayne would soon discover when she went to her suite and found her luggage had been moved to their penthouse. All the more reason for him to turn over control of the casino to his second in command and hotfoot it back to the penthouse. Jayne would be fired up.

A magnificent sight not to be missed.

* * *

Steamed as hell over Conrad's latest arrogant move, Jayne rode the elevator to the penthouse level, her old home. The front-desk personnel had given her a key card without hesitation or questions. Conrad had no doubt told them to expect her since he'd moved her clothes from the room she'd chosen.

Damn him.

Coming here was tough enough, and she'd planned to give herself a little distance by staying in a different suite. In addition to the penthouse, the casino had limited quarters for the most elite guests. Conrad had built a larger hotel situated farther up the hillside. It wasn't like she'd snubbed him by staying at that other hotel. Besides, their separation wasn't a secret.

She curled her toes to crack out the tension and focused on finding Conrad.

And her clothes.

The gilded doors slid open to a cavernous entryway. She steeled herself for the familiar sight of the Louis VXI reproduction chairs and hall table she'd selected with such care only to find…

Conrad had changed *everything*. She hadn't expected the place to stay completely the same since she'd left—okay, maybe she had—but she couldn't possibly have anticipated such a radical overhaul.

She stepped into the ultimate man cave, full of massive leather furniture and a monstrous television screen halfway hidden behind an oil painting that slid to the side. Even the drapes had been replaced on the wall-wide window showcasing a moonlit view of the Mediterranean. Thick curtains had been pulled open, revealing yacht lights dotting the water like stars. There was still a sense of high-end style, like the rest of the casino, but without the least hint of feminine frills.

Apparently Conrad had stripped those away when they separated.

She'd spent years putting together the French provincial decor, a blend of old-world elegance with a warmth that every home should have.

Had he torn the place apart in anger? Or had he simply not cared? She wasn't sure she even wanted to know what had happened to their old furnishings.

Right now, she only cared about confronting her soon-to-be ex-husband. She didn't have to search far.

Conrad sprawled in an oversize chair with a crystal glass in hand. A bottle of his favored Chivas Regal Royal Salute sat open on the ma-hogany table beside him. A sleek upholstered sofa had once rested there, an elegant but sturdy piece they'd made love on more than once.

On second thought, getting rid of the furniture seemed like a very wise move after all.

She hooked her purse on the antique wine rack lining the wall. Her heels sunk into the plush Moroccan rug with each angry step. "Where is my bag? I need my clothes."

"Your luggage is here in our penthouse, of course." He didn't move, barely blinked...just brooded. "Where else would it be?"

"In *my* suite. I checked into separate quarters on a different floor as you must know."

"I was informed the second you picked up your key." He knocked back the last bit of his drink.

"And you had my things moved anyway." What did he expect to gain with these games?

"I'm arrogant. Remember? You had to already know what would happen when you checked in. No matter what name you use, the staff would recognize my wife."

Maybe she had, subconsciously hoping to make a prideful statement. "Silly me for hoping my request would be honored—as your wife."

"And 'silly' me for thinking you wouldn't embarrass me in front of my own staff."

Contrition nipped at her heels. Regardless of what had happened between them near the end of their marriage, she'd loved him deeply. She was so tired of hurting him, of the pain inside her, as well.

She sank into the chair beside him, weary to her toes, needing to finish this and move on with her life, to settle down with someone wonderfully boring and uncomplicated. "I'm sorry. You're right. That was thoughtless of me."

"Why did you do it?" He set aside his glass and leaned closer. "You know there's plenty of space in the penthouse."

Even if he wouldn't offer total honesty, she could. "Because I'm scared to be alone with you."

"God, Jayne." He reached out to her, clasping her wrist with callused fingers. "I'm fifty different kinds of a bastard, but never—never, damn it—would I hurt you."

His careful touch attested to that, as well as years together where he'd always stayed in control, even during their worst arguments. She wished she had his steely rein over wayward emotions. She would give anything to hold back the flood of feelings washing over her now, threatening to drown her.

Words—honesty—came pouring out of her. "I didn't mean that. I'm afraid I won't be able to resist sleeping with you."

Two

With Jayne's agonized confession echoing in his ears and resonating deep in his gut, holding himself still was the toughest thing Conrad had ever done—other than letting Jayne go the day she'd walked out on their marriage. But he needed to think this through, and fast. One wrong move and this confrontation could blow up in his face.

Every cell in his body shouted for him to scoop her out of that leather chair, take her to his room and make love to her all night long. Hell, all weekend long. And he would have—if he believed she would actually follow through on that wish to have sex.

But he could read Jayne too clearly. While she desired him, she was still pissed off. She would change her mind about sleeping with him before he finished pulling the pins from her pale blond hair. He needed more time to wipe away her reservations and persuade her that sleeping together one last time was a good thing.

Pulling back his hand, he grabbed the bottle instead and poured another drink. "As I recall, I didn't ask you to have sex with me."

If she sat any straighter in that seat, her spine would snap. "You don't have to say the words. Your eyes seduce me with a look." Her chin quivered. "*My* eyes betray me, because when I look at you…I want you. So much."

Okay, maybe he could be persuaded not to wait after all. "Why is that a bad thing?"

A clear battle waged in her light blue eyes that he understood quite well. The past three years apart had been a unique kind of hell for him, but eventually he'd accepted that their marriage was over. He just refused to end it via a courier.

Call him stubborn, but he'd wanted Jayne to look him in the face when she called it quits. Well, he'd gotten his wish—only to have her throw him a serious curveball. She still wanted him every bit as much as he wanted her.

Granted, sex between them had always been more than good, even when they'd used it to distract them from their latest argument. One last weekend together would offer the ultimate distraction. They could cleanse away the gnawing hunger and move on. He just had to persuade her to his way of thinking

The battle continued in her eyes until, finally, she shook her head, a strand of blond hair sliding loose. "You're not going to win. Not this time." Standing, she demanded, "Give me my clothes back, and don't you dare tell me to go into our old bedroom to get them myself."

He'd been right to wait, to play it cool for now. "They're already in the guest room."

Her mouth dropped open in surprise. "Oh, I'm sorry for thinking the worst of you."

He shrugged. "Most of the time you would be right."

"Damn it, Conrad," she said softly, her shoulders lowering, her face softening, "I don't want to feel bad for you, not now. I just want your signature and peace."

"All *I* ever wanted was to make you happy." Tonight might not be the right time to indulge in tantric sex, but that didn't mean he couldn't start lobbying. He shoved to his feet, stepped closer and reached out to stroke that loose lock of hair. "Jayne, I didn't ask you to have sex, but make no mistake, I think about being with you and how damn great we were together."

Teasing the familiar texture of her hair between his fingers, he brushed back the strand, his knuckles grazing her shoulder as he tugged free the pin still hanging on. Her pupils went wide with awareness and a surge of victory pumped through him. He knew the unique swirl of her tousled updo so well he could pull the pins out of it blindfolded.

He stepped aside. "Sleep well, Jayne."

Her hands shook as she swept back the loose strand, but she didn't say a word. She spun away on her high heels and snagged her purse from the wine rack before making tracks toward the spare room. He had a feeling peace wasn't in the cards for either of them anytime soon.

Jayne closed the guest-room door behind her and sagged back, wrapping her arms around herself in a death grip to keep from throwing herself at Conrad. After three long years without him, she hadn't expected her need for him to be this strong. Her mind filled with fantasies of leaning over him as he sat in that monstrously big chair, of sliding her knees up on either side until she straddled his lap.

There was something intensely stirring about the times she'd taken charge of him, a scenario she'd half forgotten in their time apart. But she loved that feeling of sensual power. Sure, he could turn the tables in a heartbeat—a gleam in his eyes would make that clear—but then she would tug his tie free, unbutton his shirt, his pants...

She slid down the door to sit on the floor. A sigh burst free. This wasn't as easy as she'd expected.

At least she had a bed to herself without arguing, a minor victory. She looked around at the "tomato-red room" as Conrad had called it. He'd left this space unchanged and the relief she felt over such a minor point surprised her. Why did it mean so much to her that he hadn't tossed out everything from their old life?

Shoving back up to her feet, she tapped a vintage bench used as a luggage rack and skimmed her fingers along the carved footboard. He'd even kept the red toile spread and curtains. She'd wanted a comfortable space for their family to visit. Except Conrad and his older sister only exchanged birthday and Christmas cards.Since his parents and her mother had passed away, that didn't leave many relatives. Jayne definitely hadn't invited her father and his new wife…

Had she let some deep-seated "daddy issues" lead her to choose a man destined to break her heart? That was not the first time the thought had occurred to her—okay, how could she dodge the possibility when Conrad had tossed it in her face at least a dozen times? She'd forgotten how he had a knack for catching her unaware, like how he'd sent her clothes here rather than demanding she sleep in their old room.

Like the way he'd tugged the pin from her hair.

Her mind had been so full of images of them together, and she'd actually admitted how much she still wanted him. Yet, he'd turned her down even though it was clear from his eyes, from his touch—from his arousal—how much he wanted her, too. She knew his body as well as her own, but God, would she ever understand the man?

She tossed her purse on the bed and her cell phone slid out. She snatched it up only to find the screen showed three missed calls from the same number.

Guilt soured in her stomach, and how twisted was that? She wasn't actually dating Anthony Collins. She'd been careful to keep things in the "friend" realm since she'd begun Hospice care for his aged great-uncle who'd recently passed away from end stage lung cancer.

She'd seen a lot of death in her job, and it was never easy. But knowing she'd helped ease a person's final days, had helped their families as well, she could never go back to filling her time with buying furniture and planning meals. She didn't even want to return to working in an E.R.

She'd found her niche for her nursing degree.

While there were others who could cover her rounds at work, she wanted to resume the life she'd started building for herself in Miami. And to do that, she needed closure for her marriage.

She thumbed the voice mail feature and listened…

"Jayne, just checking in…" Anthony's familiar voice piped through with the sound of her French bulldog, Mimi, barking in the background since he'd agreed to dog sit for her. "How did your flight go? Call me when you get a chance."

Beep. Next message.

"I'm getting worried about you. Hope you're not stranded from a layover, at the mercy of overpriced airport food."

Beep. Next call from Anthony, he hung up without speaking.

She should phone him back. Should. But she couldn't listen to his voice, not with desire for Conrad still so hot and fresh in her veins. She took the coward's way out and opted for a text message instead.

Made it 2 Monte Carlo safely. Thanks 4 worrying. 2 tired to talk. Will call later. Give Mimi an extra treat from me.

More of that remorse still churning, she hit Send and turned off the power. Big-time coward. She pitched her phone back in her purse. The *clink* as her cell hit metal reminded her of the ring Conrad had slipped back inside. She'd won a battle by delivering the divorce papers, and she could think of plenty of charities that would benefit from a donation if—when—she sold the ring.

She may not have gotten to place her bet, but she'd won tonight. Right?

Wrong. She sagged onto the edge of the bed and stared at her monogrammed carry-on bag. Good thing she'd packed her ereader, because there wasn't a chance in hell she would be sleeping.

Parked on the glassed-in portion of his balcony, Conrad thumbed through the Zhutov document on his tablet computer.

Monte Carlo rarely slept at night anyhow, the perfect setting for a chronic insomniac like himself. Beyond the windows, yachts bobbed in the bay, lights glowing. No doubt the casino below him was still in full swing, but he'd soundproofed his quarters.

The divorce papers lay beside him on the twisted iron breakfast table. He'd already reviewed them and found them every bit as frustrating as when his lawyer had relayed the details. And yes, he knew the contents even though he'd led Jayne to believe otherwise.

She was insistent on walking away with next to nothing, just as she'd done the day she'd left. He'd already drawn up an addendum that created a trust for her, and she could do whatever the hell she wanted with the money. But he'd vowed in front of God and his peers to protect this woman for life, and he would follow through on that promise even beyond their divorce.

He hadn't made that commitment lightly.

Frustration simmered inside him, threatening his focus as he read the Zhutov report from Salvatore. He'd given up his marriage for cases like this, so he'd damn well better succeed or he would have lost Jayne for nothing.

The world was better off with that bastard behind bars. Zhutov had masterminded one of the largest counterfeiting organizations in Eurasia. He'd used that influence to shift the balance of power between countries by manipulating the strength of a country's currency. At a time when many regions were struggling for financial survival, the least dip in economics could be devastating.

And from all appearances, Zhutov had played his tricks out of an amoral need for power and a desire to advance his son's political aspirations by any means possible.

Helping Interpol stop crooks like that was more than a job. It was a road to redemption after what Conrad had done in high school. He'd committed a crime not all that different from Zhutov's and gotten off with a slap on the wrist. At the time he'd manipulated the stock market, he'd deluded himself into thinking he was some sort of dispenser of cosmic justice, stealing from the evil rich to give to the more deserving.

Utter crap.

At fifteen, he'd been old enough to know better. He'd understood the difference between right and wrong. But he'd been so caught up in his own selfish need to prove he was better than his crook of a father, he'd failed to take into account the workers and the families hurt in the process.

He might have avoided official prison time, but he still owed a debt. When Salvatore had retired as headmaster of North Carolina Military Prep and taken a job with Interpol, Conrad had been one of his first recruits. He'd worked a case cracking open an international insider trading scam.

The sound of the balcony door opening drew him back to the moment. He didn't have to turn around. Jayne's scent already drifted toward him. Her sea-breeze freshness, a natural air, brought the outdoors inside. She'd told him once she'd gotten out of the practice of wearing perfume as a nurse because scents disturbed some patients. And yes, he remembered most everything about her, such as how she usually slept like a log regardless of the time zone.

That she was restless now equaled progress. It was already past 2:00 a.m.

He shut down the file and switched to a computer game, still keeping his back to her.

"Conrad?" Her husky voice stoked his frustration higher, hotter. "What are you doing up so late?"

"Business." The screen flashed with a burst of gunfire as his avatar fought back an ambush in Alpha Realms IV.

She laughed softly, stepping farther onto the balcony silently other than the swoosh of her silky robe against her legs. "So I see. New toy from your pal Troy Donavan?"

Conrad had the inside track on video games since a fellow felonious high school bud of his now ran a lucrative computer software corporation. "It's my downtime, and I don't even have to leave town. Did you need something?"

"I was getting a glass of water, and I saw you're still awake. You always were a night owl."

More than once she'd walked up behind him, slid her arms around his neck and offered to help him relax with a massage that always led to more.

"Feel free to have a seat." He guided his avatar

around a corner in dystopian city ruins. "But I can't promise to be much of a conversationalist."

"Keep playing your game."

"Hmm…" Alpha Realms provided a safe distraction from the peripheral view of Jayne sliding onto the lounger. The way the silky robe clung to her shower-damp skin, she could have been naked.

Her legs crossed at the ankles, her fuzzy slippers dangling from her toes. "Why do you keep working when you could clearly retire?"

Because his fast-paced, wealthy lifestyle provided the perfect cover for him to move in the circles necessary to bring down crooks like Zhutov. "You knew I lived at the office when you married me."

"I was like any woman crazy in love." She cupped a water glass between her hands. "I deluded myself into believing I could change you."

He hadn't expected her to concede anything, much less that. He set aside his tablet, on top of those damn divorce papers. "I remember the first time I saw you."

The patio sconce highlighted her smile. "You were one of the crankiest, most uncooperative emergency room patients I'd ever met."

He'd been in Miami following up on a lead for Salvatore. Nothing hairy, just chasing a paper trail. He would have been back in Monte Carlo by morning, except a baggage handler at the airport dropped an overweight case on Conrad's foot. Unable to bear weight on it even when he'd tried to grit through the pain, he'd ended up in the E.R. rather than on his charter jet. And he'd still protested the entire way.

Although his mood had taken a turn for the better once the head nurse on the night shift stepped into the waiting room to find out why he'd sent everyone else running. "I'm surprised you spoke to me after what an uncooperative bastard I was."

"I still can't believe you insisted you just wanted a walking boot, that you had an important meeting you couldn't miss because of what you called a stubbed toe."

"Yeah, not my shining moment."

"Smart move sending flowers to the staff members you pissed off." She scratched the corner of her mouth with her pinky. "I don't believe I ever told you, but I thought they were for me when they arrived."

"I wanted to win you over. Apologizing to your coworkers seemed the wisest course to take." He'd extended his stay in Miami under the guise of looking into investment property.

They'd eloped three months later, in a simple ocean-side ceremony with a couple of his alumni buddies as witnesses.

Jayne sipped her water, her eyes unblinking as if she might be holding back tears. "So this is really it for us."

"Nice to know this isn't any easier for you than it is for me."

Her hand shook as she set aside her glass. "Of course this isn't easy for me. But I want it to be done. I want to move past this and be happy again."

Damn, it really got under his skin that he still hurt her even after all this time apart.

"I'm sorry you're unhappy." Back when, he would have moved heaven and earth to give her what she wanted. Now it appeared all he could give her was a divorce.

"Do you really mean that?" She swung her feet to the side, sitting on the edge of the lounger. "Or is that why you held off signing the papers for so long? So you could see me squirm?"

"Honest to God, Jayne, I just want both of us to be happy, and if that means moving on, then okay." Although she looked so damn right beside him, back in his life again. He would be haunted by the vision of her there for a long time to come. "But right now, neither of us seems to be having much luck with the concept of a clean break."

"What are you saying?"

Persuading her would take a lot more savvy than sending a few dozen roses to her friends. "I think we need to take a couple of days to find that middle ground, peace or closure or whatever the hell therapists are calling it lately."

"We've been married for seven years." She

fished into the pocket of her robe and pulled out her engagement ring and wedding band set. "How do you expect to find closure in two days when we've been trying for the last three years?"

He did not want to see those damn rings again. Not unless they were sitting where he'd put them—on her finger.

"Has ignoring each other worked for you? Because even living an ocean apart hasn't gone so well for me."

"You'll get no argument from me." Her fingers closed around the rings. "What exactly do you have in mind?"

He sensed victory within his sights. She was coming around to his way of thinking. But he had to be sure because if he miscalculated and moved too soon he could risk sending her running.

"I suggest we spend a simple night out together, no pressure. My old high school buddy Malcolm Douglas is performing nearby—in the Côte d'Azur—tomorrow night. I have tickets. Go with me."

"What if I say no?"

Not an option. He played his trump card. "Do you want my signature on those divorce papers?"

She dropped her rings on top of the computer that just happened to be resting over the divorce papers. "Are you blackmailing me?"

"Call it a trade." He rested his hand over the five-carat diamond he'd chosen for her, only her. "You give me two days and I'll give you the divorce papers. Signed."

"Just two days?" She studied him through narrowed, suspicious eyes.

He gathered up the rings and pressed them to her palm, closing her fingers over them again. "Forty-eight hours."

Forty-eight hours to romance her back into his bed one last time.

Three

Gasping, Jayne sat upright in bed, jolted out of a deep sleep by…sunlight?

Bold morning rays streamed through the part in the curtains. Late morning, not a sunrise. She looked at the bedside clock: *10:32 a.m.?* Shoving her tangled hair aside, she blinked and the time stayed the same.

Then changed to 10:33.

She never overslept and she never had trouble with jet lag, thanks to her early years in nursing working odd shifts in the emergency room. Except last night she'd had trouble falling asleep even after a long bubble bath. Restless, she'd been foolish enough to dance with temptation by talking to Conrad on a moonlit Mediterranean night.

He'd talked her into staying.

God, was she even ready to face him today with the memory of everything she'd said right there between them? The thought of him out there, a simple door away, had her so damn confused. She'd all but propositioned him, and he'd turned her down. She'd been so sure she would have to keep him at arm's length she'd checked into the room on another floor. That seemed petty, and even egotistical, now.

He'd simply wanted the common courtesy of a face-to-face goodbye and he'd been willing to wait three years to get it. The least she could do was behave maturely now. She just had to get through the next forty-eight hours without making a fool of herself over this man again.

Throwing aside the covers, she stood and came face-to-face with her reflection in the mirror. A fright show stared back at her, showcased by the gold-leaf frame. With her tousled hair and dark circles under her eyes, she looked worse than after pulling back-to-back shifts in the E.R.

Pride demanded she shower and change before facing Conrad, who would undoubtedly look hot in whatever he wore. Even bed-head suited him quite well, damn him.

A bracing shower later, she tugged on her favorite black skinny jeans and a poet's shirt belted at the waist, the best she could do with what little she had in her suitcase. But she'd expected to be traveling back to the States today, divorce papers in hand. At least she'd thought to change her flight and arrange for more time off before going to bed last night.

Nerves went wild in her chest as she opened the door. The sound of clanking silverware echoed down the hallway, the scent of coffee teasing her nose. He'd said they would spend two days finding peace with each other, but as she thought about facing him over breakfast, she felt anything but peaceful.

Still, she'd made a deal with him and she refused to let him see her shake in her shoes—or all but beg him for sex again.

Trailing her fingers down the chair railing in the hall, she made her way through the "man cave" living room and into the dining area. And oh, God, he'd swapped her elegant dining room set for the equivalent of an Irish pub table with a throne at the head. *Really?*

And where was the barbarian of the hour?

The table had been set for two, but he was nowhere to be seen. A rattle from the kitchen gave her only a second's warning before a tea cart came rolling in, but not pushed by Conrad.

A strange woman she'd never met before pushed the cart containing a plate of pastries, a bowl of fruit and two steaming carafes. At the moment, food was the last thing on Jayne's mind. Instead, at the top of the list was discovering the identity of this stranger. This beautiful redheaded stranger who looked very at ease in Conrad's home, serving breakfast from a familiar tea cart that had somehow survived the "purge of Jayne" from the premises.

Jayne thrust out her hand. "Good morning. I'm Jayne Hughes, and you would be?"

Given the leggy redhead was wearing jeans and a silk blouse, she wasn't from housekeeping.

"I'm Hillary Donavan. I'm married to Conrad's friend."

"Troy Donavan, the computer mogul who went to high school with Conrad." The pieces fell into place and, good Lord, did she ever feel ridiculous. "I saw your engagement and wedding announcements in the tabloids. You're even lovelier in person."

Hillary crinkled her nose. "That's a very polite way of saying I'm not photogenic. I hate the cameras, and I'm afraid they reciprocate."

The photos hadn't done her justice, but by no means could Hillary Donavan ever look anything but lovely—and happy. The newlywed glow radiated from her, leaving Jayne feeling weary and more than a little sad over her own lost dreams.

She forced a smile on her face. "I assume that breakfast is for us?"

"Why yes, it is," Hillary answered, sweeping the glass cover from the pastries. "Cream cheese filled, which I understand is your favorite, along with chocolate mint tea for you and coffee for me."

And big fat strawberries. All of her favorites.

She couldn't help but dig to find out who'd thought to make that happen. "How lovely of the kitchen staff to remember my preferences."

"Um, actually…" Hillary parked the cart between two chairs and waved for Jayne to sit. "I'm a former event planner so nosy habits die hard. I asked Conrad, and he was wonderfully specific."

He remembered, all the way down to the flavor of hot tea, when he'd always preferred coffee, black, alongside mounds of food. As she stared at the radically different decor, she wondered how many other times he'd deferred to her wishes and she just hadn't known.

Jayne touched the gold band around a plate from her wedding china. "I didn't realize you and your husband live in Monte Carlo now."

"Actually we flew over for a little unofficial high school reunion to see Malcolm's charity concert tonight. Word is he's sold out, set to take the Côte d'Azur by storm."

They were all going in a group outing? She felt like a girl who thought she'd been asked to the movie only to find out the whole class was going along. How ironic when she'd so often wished they had more married friends.

"I have to confess to having a fan girl moment the first time I met Malcolm Douglas in person." Hillary poured coffee from the silver carafe, the java scent steaming up all the stronger with reminders of breakfasts with Conrad. "I mean, wow, to have drinks and shoot the breeze with the latest incarnation of Harry Connick, Jr. or Michael Bublé? Pretty cool. Oh, and I'm supposed to tell you that evening gowns are being sent up this afternoon for you to choose from, since you probably packed light and it's a black-tie charity event. But I'm rambling. Hope you don't mind that I'm barging in on you."

"I'm glad for the company. Not many of Conrad's friends are married." When Troy had come to visit, she'd wished for a gal pal to hang out with and now she finally had one…too late for it to matter. "And when we were together, none of his classmates had walked down the aisle yet."

"They're getting to that age now. Even Elliot Starc got engaged recently." She shook her head laughing. "Another bad boy with a heart of gold. Did you ever get to meet him?"

"The one who was sent to the military high school after too many arrests for joy riding." Although according to Conrad, the joy riding had been more like car theft, but Elliot had influential friends. "Now he races cars on the international circuit."

"That's the one. Nobody thought he would ever settle down." Hillary's farm fresh quality, her uncomplicated friendliness, was infectious. "But then who would have thought my husband, the Robin Hood Hacker, would become Mr. Domesticity?"

The Robin Hood Hacker had infiltrated the Department of Defense's system, exposing corruption. After which, he'd ended up at North Carolina Military Prep reform school with Conrad. Malcolm Douglas had joined them later, having landed a plea bargain in response to drug charges.

Taking their histories into account, maybe she'd been wrong to think she could tame the bad boy. Was Hillary Donavan in for the same heartbreak down the road?

Shaking her head, Jayne cut into the pastry, cream cheese filling oozing out. "You're not at all what I expected when I read Troy got married."

"What *did* you expect?"

"Someone less...normal." She'd always felt so alone in Conrad's billionaire world. She hadn't imagined finding a friend like the neighbors she'd grown up with. "I seem to be saying all the wrong things. I hope you didn't take that the wrong way."

"No offense taken, honestly. Troy is a bit eccentric, and I'm, well, not." She twisted her diamond and emerald wedding ring, smiling contentedly. "We balance each other."

Jayne had once thought the same thing about herself and Conrad. She was a romantic, and he was so brooding. Looking back now, she'd assumed because of his high school years he was some sort of tortured soul and her nurse's spirit yearned to heal him.

Silverware clinked on the china as they ate and the silence stretched. She felt the weight of Hillary's curious stare and unspoken question.

Jayne lifted her cup of tea. "You can go ahead and ask."

"Sorry to be rude." Hillary set aside her fork, a strawberry still speared on the end. "I'm just surprised to see you and Conrad together. I hope this means you've patched things up."

"I'm afraid not. The divorce will be final soon." How much, if anything, had he shared with his friends about the breakup? "We had some final paperwork to attend to. And while I'm here, I guess we're both trying to prove we can be civil to each other. Which is crazy since our paths will never cross again."

"You never know."

"I do know. Once I leave here, my life and Conrad's will go in two very different directions." Jayne folded her napkin and placed it on the table, her appetite gone.

She couldn't even bring herself to be mad at Hillary for being nice and happy. And Jayne hoped deep in her heart that Troy would be the bad boy who'd changed for the woman he'd married.

She'd been certain Conrad had changed, too, but he'd been so evasive about his travels, refusing to be honest with her when she'd confronted him again and again about his mysterious absences. He didn't disappear often, but when he did, he didn't leave a note or contact her. His excuses when he returned were thin at best. She'd wanted to believe he wasn't like his father…or her father. She still wanted to believe that.

But she couldn't be a fool. He kept insisting she should trust him. Well, damn it, he should have trusted her. The fact that he didn't left her with only two conclusions.

He wasn't the man she'd hoped, and he'd very likely never really loved her at all.

This little fantasy two-day make-nice-a-thon was just that. A fantasy. Thank God, he'd turned her away last night, because had she fallen into bed with him, she would have regretted it fiercely come morning time. Her body and her brain had never been *simpatico* around her husband.

But she had a great big broken heart as a reminder to listen only to her common sense.

Common sense told him that keeping his distance today would give him an edge tonight. But staying away from Jayne now that she'd returned to Monte Carlo was driving him crazy.

Seeing her on the security camera feed from the solarium didn't help his restraint, either.

But the secure room offered the safest place for him to hang out with a couple of his high school buds—Donavan and Douglas—who'd also been recruited for Interpol by Colonel Salvatore. The colonel had his own little army of freelancers drafted from the ranks of his former students. Although God knows why he'd chosen them, the least conformist boys in the whole school. But they were tight with each other, bonded by their experiences trying to patch their lives back together.

They'd even dubbed themselves "The Alpha Brotherhood." They could damn well conquer anything.

Now, they shared a deeper bond in their work for Salvatore. For obvious reasons, they still couldn't talk freely out in public. But a vaulted security room in his casino offered a place of protected privacy so they could let their guards down.

The remains of their lunch lay scattered on the table. Normally he would have enjoyed the hell out of this. Not today. His thoughts stayed too firmly on Jayne, and his hand gravitated toward her image on the screen.

Donavan tipped back his chair, spinning his

signature fedora on one finger. "Hey, Conrad, I picked up some great Cuban smokes last week, but I wouldn't want to start Malcolm whining that his allergies are acting up."

Douglas scratched at the hole in the knees of his jeans. "I do not whine."

"Okay—" Donavan held up his hands "—if that's the story you want to go with, fine, I'm game."

"I am seriously going to kick the crap out of you—" Douglas had picked fights from day one "—just for fun."

"Bring it."

"I would, but I don't want to risk straining my vocal cords and disappoint the groupies." Douglas grinned just like he was posing for the cover of one of his CDs. "But then, you've been benched by marriage so you wouldn't understand."

Some things never changed. They could have all been in their barracks, seventeen years ago. Except today Conrad didn't feel much like joining in. His eyes stayed locked on the screen showing security feed from his place.

Or more precisely, his eyes stayed locked on Jayne at the indoor pool with Donavan's wife. He couldn't take his eyes off the image of her relaxed and happy. Jayne wore clothes instead of a swimsuit, not that it mattered when he could only think of her wearing nothing at all. She was basking in the sun through the solarium windows.

Donavan sailed his hat across the room, Frisbee style, nailing Conrad in the shoulder. "Are you doing okay, brother?"

Conrad plucked the hat from the floor and tossed it on the table alongside his half-eaten bowl of ratatouille. "Why wouldn't I be?"

"Oh, I don't know…" Malcolm lowered his chair legs to the ground again. "Maybe because your ex-wife is in town and you haven't stopped looking at her on that video monitor since we got in here."

"She's not my ex-wife yet." He resisted the

urge to snap and further put a damper on their lunch. "Anybody up for a quick game of cards?"

Donavan winced. "So you can clean me out again?"

Malcolm hauled his chair back to the table. "Now who's whining?"

Pulling his eyes if not his attention off Jayne, Conrad swept aside the dishes and reached for a deck of cards.

Between their freelance work for Interpol and their regular day jobs, there was little time left to hang out like they'd done during the old days. Damn unlucky for him one of those few occasions happened to be now, when they were all around to witness the final implosion of his marriage.

And what if he didn't get one last night with Jayne? What if he had to spend the rest of his life with this hunger gnawing at his gut every time a blonde woman walked by? Except no woman, regardless of her hair color, affected him the way Jayne did.

No matter what he told his brothers, he was

not okay. But damn it, he would be tonight after the concert when he lay Jayne back on that sofa and made her his again.

Jayne hadn't been on a date in three years, not even to McDonald's with a friend. How ironic that her first post-separation outing with a man would be with her own estranged husband. And he'd taken her to a black-tie charity concert on the Côte d'Azur—the French Riviera.

Although she had to admit, his idea of finding a peaceful middle ground had merit—even if he'd all but blackmailed her to gain her cooperation.

At least seated in the historic opera house she could lose herself in the crowd, simply sit beside Conrad and enjoy the music, without worrying about temptation or messy conversations. Malcolm Douglas sang a revamp of some 1940s tune, accompanying his vocals on the grand piano. His smooth baritone voice washed over her as effortlessly as the glide of Conrad's fingers on her shoulder. So what if her husband had draped his arm along the back of her seat? No big deal.

In fact, she'd been surprised at how little pressure he'd put on her throughout the day, especially after their intense discussions, their potent attraction, the night before. Waking up alone was one thing. But then to have him spend the entire day away from her...

His amenability was good. Wasn't it?

That niggling question had grown during the rest of the afternoon without him. Lunchtime passed and she started to question if she'd heard his offer of a date correctly. Except Hillary had mentioned it, as well. Then the staff brought a selection of evening wear in her size. She'd chosen a silver gown with bared shoulders, the mild winter only requiring a black satin wrap.

By the time Conrad arrived at their suite to pick her up, her nerves had been strung so tightly, she was ready to jump out of her skin. The sight of him in a tuxedo, broad shoulders filling out the coat to mouthwatering perfection, had just been downright unfair. All the way to the limo, she'd thought he would make his move, only to find Troy and Hillary Donavan waiting in the limousine, ready to go out to dinner with them before the concert. But then hadn't Hillary said Troy and Conrad were having some kind of reunion?

The evening had been perfect.

And perfectly frustrating.

Conrad's thumb grazed the sensitive crook of her neck, along the throb of her pulse. Did he know her heart beat faster for him? Her breath hitched in her throat.

Hillary leaned toward her and whispered, "Are you all right?"

Wincing, Jayne resisted the urge to shove Conrad's arm away. "I'm fine, just savoring."

Savoring the feel of Conrad's hand on her bare skin.

Damn it.

He shifted in his seat, his fingers stroking along the top of her arm and sending shivers along her spine. She struggled not to squirm in her seat and draw Hillary's attention again. But that was getting tougher and tougher to manage by the second. He had to know what he was doing.

Still, if he'd been trying to seduce her, he could have been a lot more overt, starting with ditching the other couple. Her mind filled with vivid memories of the time he'd reserved a private opera box for a performance of *La Bohème* and made love to her with his hand under her dress.

Only one of the many times he'd diverted an argument with sex.

Yet now, he turned her down. Why?

The lights came up for intermission, and Conrad's arm slid away as he applauded. She bit her lip to keep from groaning.

He stood then angled back down to her. "Do you and Hillary mind keeping each other company while Troy and I talk shop? He's developing some new software to prevent against hackers at the casino."

"Of course I don't mind." She'd given up the right to object when she'd walked out on him three years ago. Soon, their breakup would be official and legal.

"Thanks," he said, cupping her face in a warm palm for an instant before straightening. At the last second, he glanced back over his shoulder. "I didn't think it was possible, but you look even more beautiful than the night we saw *La Bohème*."

Her mouth fell open.

The reference to that incredible night had been no accident. Conrad had known exactly what he was doing. No doubt, her savvy husband had planned his every move all day with the express purpose of turning her inside out. The only question that remained?

Had he done so just for the satisfaction of turning her down again? Or did he want to ensure she wouldn't back away at the last second?

Either way, two could play that game.

Four

Conrad downshifted his Jaguar as he took the curve on the coastal road, Jayne in the passenger seat.

After the concert ended, he'd sent Troy and Hillary off in the limo, his Jaguar already parked and waiting for the next part of his plan to entice Jayne. She'd always loved midnight rides along the shore and since neither of them seemed able to sleep much, this longer route home seemed the right idea for his campaign to win her over.

When he took her back to the penthouse, he wanted to make damn sure they were headed straight for bed. Or to the rug in front of the fireplace.

Hell, against the wine rack was fine by him as long as he had Jayne naked and in his arms. The day apart after the fireworks last night seemed to have worked the way he'd hoped, giving the passion time to simmer. Even after three years away from each other, he understood the sensual side of her at least.

He glanced over at her, moonlight casting a glow around her as she toyed with her loose blond hair brushing her shoulders. His fingers itched to comb through the silky strands. Soon, he promised himself, looking back at the winding cliff road. Very soon.

She touched his arm lightly. "Are you sure you wouldn't rather visit with Malcolm tonight?"

Instead of being with her?

Not a chance.

"And steal Malcolm away from his groupies?" He kept his hand on the gearshift, enjoying the feel of her touch on him. Too bad the dash lights shone on her empty ring finger. "Even I wouldn't be that selfish."

"If you're certain." Her hand trailed away, searing him with a ghostly caress.

His hand twitched as he shifted into fourth. He winced at the slight grind to the finely tuned machine. "We had a chance to shoot the breeze this afternoon with Troy."

"Malcolm seems so different when he's away from the spotlight." She stretched her legs out in front of her, kicking off her silvery heels and wriggling her painted toes under the light blast of the heater. "It's difficult to reconcile the guy in holey blue jeans jamming on the guitar in your living room to the slick performer in suits and ties, crooning from the piano."

"Whatever gets the job done." He forced his eyes back on the road before he drove them over a cliff. "You and Hillary seem to have hit it off."

"I enjoyed the day with her, and it was nice to have another woman's opinion when I picked out which dress to wear tonight." She trailed her thumb along her bared collarbone, her black wrap having long ago slipped down around her waist.

The silver gown glistened in the glow of the

dash, all but begging him to pull over and devote his undivided attention to peeling off the fitted bodice.…

Eyes on the road.

He guided the Jag around another curve, yacht lights glinting on the water far below.

She angled her head to the side. "What are you thinking about?"

Nuh-uh. Not answering that one. "What are *you* thinking about?"

"Um, hello?" She laughed dryly. "Exactly what you intended for me to think about. The night we went to see *La Bohème.*"

How neatly she'd turned the tables on him.

He liked that about her, the way she took control, too, which reminded him of how she'd seduced him in his favorite chair once they'd gotten home from *La Bohème.* "That was a, uh, memorable evening."

"Not everything about our marriage was bad," she conceded.

"Italian opera will always hold a special place in my heart."

Except he'd thrown out that damn chair when she left, then found he had to pitch most of the rest of his furniture as well, including the dining-room table, which also held too many sensual memories of her making her way panther-style toward him with a strawberry in her mouth. The only place they'd never made love was in that tomato-red room since she'd said it was meant for guests, which somehow made it off-limits for sex.

She inched her wrap back up and around her shoulders, the night having dipped to fifty de-grees. "I thought *Don Giovanni* was your favor-ite opera."

"The story of a hero landing in hell for his sins?" Appropriate. "A longtime favorite. Al-though I'm surprised you remember that I liked it."

"You remembered that I prefer cream cheese pastries and chocolate mint tea for breakfast."

He'd made a mental note of many things she liked back then, working his ass off to keep her happy as he felt their marriage giving way like a sandy cliff. "We were together for four years. I intended to be with you for the rest of my life."

"And you think I didn't?" Pain coated her words, as dark as the clouds shifting over the stars. "I wanted to build a family with you."

Another of her dreams he'd crushed. The ways he'd failed this woman just kept piling on, compacting his frustration until he was ready to explode.

Not trusting himself to drive, he pulled off the road and into a deserted rest area. He set the emergency brake and wished the anger inside him was as easy to halt. Anger at himself. "I gave you a puppy, damn it."

"I wanted a baby."

"Okay…" He angled toward her, half hoping she would slap his face, anything but stare at him with tears in her eyes. "Let's make a baby."

She flattened her hands to his chest, hard, stopping just shy of that slap he'd hoped for. Although a telltale flex of her jaw relayed her rising temper. "Don't you dare mock me or my dreams. That's not fair."

"I'm very serious about being with you."

"So you stay away from me all day?" she shouted, her fingers twisting in the lapels of his tuxedo. "You stay away for three whole years?"

Her question stopped him cold. "That bothered you?"

"For three years you ignored my attempts to contact you." She shoved free and leaned against the door, arms crossed under her breasts, which offered too beautiful a view. "Did you or did you not manipulate me on purpose today?"

He chose his words carefully, determined to get through the tough stuff so they could make love without the past hovering over them. "I figured we both needed space after last night if there was any chance of us enjoying our evening together."

"That makes sense," she conceded.

"I'm a logical man." He rested a hand on the back of her seat, his fingers dangling a whisper away from her hair. He was so damn close to having her, he could already taste her.

"You may think you're logical, but I don't understand half of what you do, Conrad. I do know that if you'd really loved me, truly wanted to stay married, you would have been honest. Whatever game you're playing now, it has nothing to do with love." Words tumbled from her faster and faster as if overflowing from a bottle. "You just don't want to lose. I'm another prize, a contest, a challenge. The way you've played me today and for three years? It's a game to you."

"I can assure you," he said softly, his fingers finally—thank God—finally skimming along her silky hair. "I consider the stakes to be very high. I am not in the mood to play."

"Then what are you doing? Because this back and forth, this torment, has nothing to do with peace."

"I have to agree." He traced her ear, down to the curve of her neck.

Her eyes slid closed and the air all but crackled. "Are you doing this to make me stay?"

"I told you what I want. A chance for us to say goodbye." He thumbed the throbbing pulse along her neck, his body going hard at the thought of her heart beating faster for him. "Leaving was your choice, not mine, but after three years I get that you mean business."

Her lashes fluttered open, her blue eyes pinning him. "And you really accept my decision."

"You *were* yelling at me about thirty seconds ago." He outlined her lips, her breath hot against his palm.

"Are you accusing me of being a shrew?" She nipped his finger.

He forgot to breathe. "I would never say that."

"Why not? I've called you a bastard and worse."

"I am a bastard, and I am far worse." He took her face in both hands, willing her to hear him, damn it, to finally understand how much she'd meant to him. "But I'm also a man who would have been there for you every day of your life."

She searched his eyes, her mouth so close to his their breaths tangled together. Something in her expression stopped him.

"Every day, Conrad? Unless it's one of the times you can't be reached or when you call but your number is blocked."

Damn it. He pulled away, slumping back in his seat. "I have work and holdings around the world."

"You're a broken record," she said, her voice weary and mad all at once. "But who am I to judge? You're not the only one who can keep secrets."

A chill iced the heat right out of the air. "What the hell does that mean?"

"Do you know what finally pushed me over the edge?" Her eyes filled with tears that should have been impossible to hold back. "What made me walk out?"

"It took me a couple of days to return your calls, and you'd had enough." He'd fired the secretary that hadn't put her calls through. He'd honestly been working at being more accessible to Jayne.

"Seven days, Conrad. Seven." She jabbed a finger at him, her voice going tight and the first tear sliding down her cheek. "I called you because I needed you. I'd gotten a suspicious report back on a mammogram, and the doctor wanted to do a biopsy right away."

Her words sucker punched *everything* out of him, leaving him numb. Then scared as hell.

He shot upright and started to grab her shoulders, only to hold back at the last second, afraid to touch her and upset her even more. "God, Jayne, are you all right? If I had known…"

"But you didn't." She pushed his hands away slowly, deliberately. "And don't worry, I'm fine. The lump was benign, but it sure would have been nice to have you hold my hand that week. So don't tell me you would have been there for me every day of my life. It's simply not true."

The sense of how badly he'd let Jayne down slammed over him. He closed his eyes, head back on his seat as he fought down the urge to leap out of the car and shout, punch a wall, anything to ease the crushing weight of how he'd let her down.

One deep breath at a time, he regained his composure enough to turn his head and look at her again. "What happened to the puppy?"

"Huh?" She scrubbed the backs of her hands across her wet cheeks.

"What did you do with Mimi after you left?" Mimi, named for the heroine in *La Bohème.*

"Oh, I kept Mimi, of course. She's with…a dog sitter."

Of course she'd kept the dog. Jayne wasn't the kind of person to throw away the good things in her life. He was.

He pinched the bridge of his nose, stared out the window at the churning night sea below and wished those murky waters held some answers. Jayne's ocean-fresh scent gave him only a second's warning before she took his face in her hands and kissed him.

Desperate to forget the past, Jayne sealed her lips to Conrad's. Right or wrong, she just needed to lose herself in the feel of his body against hers. The roar of the waves crashing against the shore echoed the elemental restlessness inside her.

With a low growl, he wrapped his strong, muscled arms around her. He took her mouth as thoroughly as she took his. The taste of coffee from dinner mingled with the flavor of him. And what a mix of the familiar and a first kiss wrapped up in one delicious moment. Goose bumps sprinkled along her arms, shimmering through her, as well.

Her hands slid from the warm bristle of his face to his shoulders and she held on. Because, God, this was what she'd wanted since the second she'd sensed him walk up behind her in the casino, drawn by the intoxicating warmth and bay rum scent of him. The way his hands smoothed back her hair, stroked along her arms, stoked a familiar heat inside her. She'd been right to instigate this. Here, in his arms, she didn't have to think about the pain of the past. To hell with peace and resolving their problems. Rehashing old issues just brought more pain. She wanted this bliss.

And then goodbye.

His mouth trekked to her jaw as he dipped lower, his late-day beard a sweet abrasion against her neck. Her head lolled to the side, a moan rolling up her throat. She stroked along the fine texture of his tux over bold muscles, up and into his hair. Combing through his impossibly soft strands, she urged him to give more, take more. She tugged gently, bringing his mouth back to hers.

Bittersweet pleasure rippled through her, reminding her how good they'd been together. Her breasts ached for his touch and she wriggled to get nearer, pressing against the hard wall of his chest. She struggled to get closer, swinging a knee over and bumping the gearshift.

"Damn it," Conrad's muffled curse whispered against her mouth but the thought that he might stop was more than she could bear.

She shoved her hands under his tuxedo coat, sinking her fingernails into the fine fibers of his shirt. Three years of being without sex—without *him*—crested inside her, demanding she follow through. His hand skimmed up her leg, tunneling under her dress as he'd done years ago. The rasp of his calluses along her skin ignited a special kind of pleasure and the promise of more.

Except that private theater box had been a lot

roomier than his Jaguar. And she wanted more than just his *hands* on her.

"Take me…" she gasped.

"I intend to do just that." His voice rumbled in his chest, vibrating against her.

"Not here. Home. Take me home."

He angled back to look at her as if gauging the risk of pausing. He grazed his knuckles along her cheek. "Are you sure?"

"Absolutely." As sure as anyone could be about making love with the person who'd broken her heart. She scored her nails down his back. "I know what I want. I won't change my mind about being with you tonight."

It wasn't a matter of winning or losing anymore. It was just a matter of stopping the ache and praying for some of that peace. Because wanting him was tearing her apart.

Angling into him, she nipped his bottom lip. "Conrad, I think it's time we break in your new furniture."

Conrad hauled Jayne into the private elevator and willed the doors to close faster. He may have hoped to clear the air of past issues during their drive before jumping right to sex, but now that Jayne had taken that decision out of his hands, he was all in.

He'd made record time driving back to the casino, determined to get to the penthouse before she changed her mind. God help him—both of them—if she backed out now. After tasting her again, touching her again, he was on fire from wanting to be with her. Wanting to bury himself heart deep inside her until they both forgot about everything but how damn good they were together.

Until in some way he made up for how deeply he'd let Jayne down.

He jammed his key card into the slot and the elevator doors slid closed. The mirrored walls reflected multiple images of his wife, tousled and so damn beautiful she took his breath away.

"Come here, now," she demanded, taking control in that way that turned him inside out. She grabbed his jacket and tugged him to her.

"You've been tormenting me all night with the way you look at me."

He pressed her against the cool wall as the elevator lifted. "You've been tormenting me since the day I met you."

"What are we going to do about that?" She arched against him, her hips a perfect fit against his.

"I suggest we keep right on doing this until we can figure out how we're ever going to quit." He angled his mouth over hers, teasing her with light brushes and gentle tugs on her bottom lip.

"That makes absolutely no sense," she whispered between kisses.

Nothing about the way he felt for her made a damn bit of sense. But then he'd wanted her since the first time he saw her. That had never changed, never lightened up. He gathered her hair in his hand and—

"Conrad," she gasped, "stop the elevator."

"You want me to *stop?*" Denial spiked through him.

"No, I want you to stop the elevator—" she

kissed him "—between floors—" stroked him "—so we don't have to wait a second longer."

He slapped the elevator button.

Jayne opened her arms, and he didn't even have to think. He thrust his hands into her hair, the familiar glide of those silky strands against his skin as arousing as always. Images scrolled through his mind of her slithering the blond mass over his chest as she nibbled her way down, down, down farther still until her mouth closed around him... Desire pounded in his ears in time with the bass beat of the elevator music.

As if she heard his thoughts, understood his need to have her touch him again, her fingers grazed down the front of his pants, rubbing along the length of him until he thought he would come right then and there. He gripped her wrist and eased her hand away. Soon, he promised himself, soon they could have it all.

Her hips rocked against him, and he pressed his thigh between her legs, rewarded by her breathy moan of pleasure. The gauzy length of her gown offered little barrier between him and the hot core of her.

Memories of that night at *La Bohème* seared his brain and fueled his imagination. He bunched up her dress in his fist, easing the fabric up her creamy-white legs until he reached the top of her thighs. Only a thin scrap of satin stayed between him and his goal. Between him and her.

They were completely alone in the privacy of his domain. And even if someone dared step into his realm, he shielded her with his body. Never would he leave her vulnerable to anyone or anything. She was his to protect, to cherish.

To please.

He tucked a finger into the thin string along the side and twisted until…the fabric gave way. She purred into his mouth and angled toward his touch. He wadded the panties in his fist and stuffed the torn scrap into his pocket before returning to her.

Stroking from her knee to her thigh again, he nudged her dress up until his fingers found her sweet, moist cleft. He stroked along her lips, swollen with the passion he'd given her. Without rushing, he stroked and explored, giving her time to grow accustomed to his touch, to let her desire build while he kissed her, murmuring against her mouth how damn much she drove him crazy. His other hand cupped the perfect curve of her bottom and lifted her toward the glide of his caress.

Her gasps grew faster, heavier, the rise and fall of her breasts against his chest making him throb to be inside her. He slipped two fingers into the hot dampness of her, the velvety walls already pulsing around him with the first beginnings of her orgasm. He knew her body, every telltale sign. His fingers still buried deep within her, he pressed his palm against the tight nub of nerves and circled. She writhed against him in response, gasping for him not to stop, she was so close...

He burned to drop to his knees to finish her with his mouth, to fill his senses with the essence of her, but he didn't dare risk leaving her that exposed unless they were behind locked doors. But soon, before the night was over he would make love to her with more than his hand. He would bring her to shattering completion again and again, watching the bliss play across her face.

Her head fell back against the glassed wall, her hands clamped to his shoulders, her nails digging deep. He grazed his mouth along the throbbing pulse in her neck just as she arched in his arms. Her cries of completion echoed in the confines of the elevator, blending with the music drifting from the speakers. And he watched— God, how he watched—every nuance on her beautiful face, her eyes closed, her mouth parted with panting gasps. The tip of her tongue peeked out to run along her top lip and he throbbed impossibly harder. For her. Always for her.

Her body began to slide as she relaxed in the aftermath, her arms slipping around his neck. He palmed her back, bringing her against him, although his feet weren't as steady as he would like right now. The music grew louder, sweeping into a crescendo until…

An alarm pierced his ears, jolting through him. No wait, that was the floor lifting again, the elevator rising.

"Conrad?" Her eyes blinked open, passion-fogged.

He understood the feeling well.

His head fell to rest against the mirrored wall. "That's the backup system in case the elevator breaks."

"Oh…" She froze against him then wriggled, smoothing her gown back in place. "That would have been really embarrassing if we hadn't noticed and the doors had just opened."

"This is only a temporary delay." He cupped her head and kissed her soundly before stepping into the penthouse.

She kicked her shoes off, her eyes still steamy blue, her pupils wide with desire. He flung her wrap over the wine rack and backed her down the hall. Except he didn't intend to stop at the chair or in front of the fireplace. He wanted his wife in his bed again. Where they both belonged.

Later, he would figure out why the notion of

one weekend suddenly didn't seem like near enough time with her.

He reached for the light switch only to realize…

Crap. The chandelier was already glowing overhead and he always turned the lights off when he left. Cleaning staff never came at night.

How had he let his instincts become so dulled that he'd missed the warning signs?

Someone was in his penthouse, and he should have noticed right away. His lapse could put Jayne in danger, and all because he'd let himself get carried away making out with her in an elevator. His guilt fired so hot her panties damn near burned a hole in his pocket. He moved fast, tucking her behind him as he scoped the living area and found his intruder.

Wearing his signature gray suit and red tie, Colonel Salvatore lounged in a chair in front of the fireplace, a cell phone in hand.

Conrad's old headmaster and current Interpol handler set aside his phone and stood, his scowl deeper than usual. "Conrad, we have a problem."

Five

Her head still fogged from her explosive reaction to Conrad in the elevator, Jayne stared in confusion at their unexpected guest sitting in the living room like family. She recognized Conrad's old headmaster and knew they'd kept in touch over the years, but not to the extent that the man could just waltz into their home while they were out.

Conrad's home, she reminded herself. Not hers. Not anymore.

Had her almost-ex-husband grown closer to Colonel Salvatore over the past three years? So much time had passed, even though their attraction hadn't changed one bit, it wasn't surprising there might be things she didn't know about his life anymore.

Although that wouldn't stop her from asking.

Praying she didn't look as mussed as she felt, she walked deeper into the living room, all too aware of her bare feet and hastily tossed aside heels. Not to mention the fact that she wasn't wearing panties. "Colonel Salvatore? There's something wrong?"

Conrad stepped between them, his broad back between her and their "guest." He stuffed his hands into his tuxedo pockets only to pull them back out hastily. "Jayne, I'm sorry to leave, but Colonel Salvatore and I need to talk privately. Colonel? If you'll join me downstairs in my office…"

Except Salvatore didn't move toward the door. "This concerns your wife and her safety."

Safety? Unease skittered up her spine, icing away the remnants of passion from the elevator. If this problem involved her, she wasn't going anywhere. "Whoa, hold on. I am completely confused. What does your being here for some kind of problem have to do with me?"

The colonel looked at Conrad pointedly. "You need to tell her. Everything."

Conrad's shoulders braced. His jaw went hard with a familiar stubborn set. The tender lover of moments prior was nowhere to be seen now. "Sir, with all due respect, you and I should speak alone first."

"I wouldn't advise leaving her here by herself, even for us to talk." Salvatore's serious tone couldn't be missed or ignored. "The time for discretion has passed. She needs to know. Now."

Jayne looked from man to man like watching a tennis match. Something big was going on here, something she was fast beginning to realize would fundamentally change her life. The chill of apprehension spread as her legs folded. She didn't know what scared her more—the fact that this man thought she was in serious danger, or that she could be on the verge of finally learning something significant about her ultra-secretive husband. She sat on the edge of Conrad's massive leather chair, her bare toes curling into the Moroccan carpet.

Muscles twitching and flexing with restraint under his tux jacket, Conrad parked himself by the fireplace. He didn't sit, but he didn't protest or leave, either. Whatever John Salvatore wanted of Conrad, apparently he intended to follow through. The way the colonel issued orders spoke of something more official, almost like a boss and employee relationship, which made no sense at all.

"Jayne," Conrad started, scratching along the same bristled jaw she'd stroked only minutes earlier, "my lifestyle with the casinos gives me accessibility to high-profile people. It provides me with the ability to travel around the world, without raising any questions. Sometimes, authorities use that ability to get information."

"Accessibility to what? Which authorities? What kind of information?" Her mind swirled, trying to grasp where he was going with this and what it had to do with some kind of threat. "What are you talking about?"

Salvatore clasped his hands behind his back and rocked on his heels. "I work for Interpol headquarters in Lyon, France, recruiting and managing agents around the world."

"You work for Interpol," she said slowly, realization detonating inside her as she looked at her husband, all those unexplained absences making sense for the first time. "*You* work for Interpol."

All those years, he hadn't been cheating on her. And he hadn't been following in his criminal father's footsteps. But she didn't feel relieved. Even now, he was ready to make love to her with such a huge secret between them.

Anger and betrayal scoured through her as she thought of all the times he'd looked her in the face while hiding such intense secrets. For that matter, he wouldn't have confided in her even now if his boss hadn't demanded it. She'd had a right to know at least something about a part of Conrad's life that affected her profoundly. But he'd rather ditch their marriage than give her the least inkling about his secret agent double life.

To think, she'd been a kiss away from tearing

her clothes the rest of the way off and jumping back in bed with him, even though he hadn't changed one bit. Even now the moist pleasure lingered between her legs, reminding her of how easily she'd opened for him all over again. Part of her hoped he would deny what she'd said, come up with some very, very believable explanation.

Except, damn him, he simply nodded before he turned back to John Salvatore. "Colonel, can we get back to Jayne's safety?"

"We have reason to believe the subject of your most recent investigation may have stumbled on your identity, perhaps through a mole in our organization. He's angry, and he wants revenge."

Salvatore's veiled explanation floated around her brain as she tried to piece together everything and figure out what it had to do with her husband. "Who exactly is after Conrad?"

They exchanged glances and before they could toss out some "need to know" phrase, she pressed on. "If I'm uninformed that puts us both in more danger. How can I be careful if I don't even know what to be careful about?"

Salvatore cleared his throat. "Have you heard of a man named Vladik Zhutov?"

Her heart stopped for three very stunned seconds. "Of course I've heard about him. He was all over the news. He's responsible for a major counterfeiting ring. He single-handedly tried to manipulate some small country's currency to affect the outcome of an election. But he's in jail now. Isn't he?"

The colonel dabbed his forehead with a handkerchief. "Even in prison, he has influence and connections, and we have reason to fear he might be trying to use those against Conrad."

She flattened her hand to the nearest chair to keep her legs from giving way underneath her. Her husband had always been so intent on separating himself from anything to do with his father's world. Even though his parents were both dead, Conrad wouldn't even visit their graves.

Was he on a vendetta of his own? Had he placed his life at risk to see that through?

Anger at Conrad took a backseat to fear for his safety. Her stomach knotted in horror, terror and a total denial of the possibility of a world without Conrad's indomitable presence. "Are you saying this individual has taken out some kind of hit on Conrad?"

She looked back and forth from the two men, both so stoic, giving away little in their stony expressions. How could someone stay this cool when her whole world was crumbling around her? Then she saw the pulse throbbing in Conrad's temple, a flash of something in his eyes that looked remarkably like…raw rage.

Salvatore sat on the chair beside her, angling toward her in his first sign of any kind of human softening. "Mrs. Hughes—Jayne—I'm afraid it's more complicated than that. Intelligence indicates Zhutov has been in contact with assassins, ones who are very good at what they do. They understand the best way to get revenge is to go after what means the most to that person. You, my dear, are Conrad's Achilles' heel."

Conrad was certain his head would explode before the night was through. What more could life catapult at him in one weekend?

The thought that someone—*anyone*—would dare use Jayne to get back at him damn near sent him into a blind rage. Only the need to protect her kept him in check.

Later, he would deal with the inevitable fallout from Salvatore ignoring Conrad's request to shield Jayne from the messiness of his Interpol work. He could think of a half-dozen different ways this could have been handled, all of which involved *not* telling Jayne secrets that could only put her in more danger.

Since Salvatore had dropped his "Achilles' heel" bombshell, the colonel had taken charge as he did so well. He'd shown Jayne his Interpol identification and offered to fly her to headquarters in Lyon, France. He would do whatever she needed to feel reassured, but it needed to happen quickly for her personal protection.

One thing was clear. They had to leave Monte Carlo. Tonight.

Salvatore continued to explain to Jayne in even, reasonable tones designed to calm. "When you make arrangements for work and for your dog, you need to give a plausible story that also will lead Zhutov's people in the wrong direction."

She twitched, but kept an admirable cool given everything she'd been told. "My phone is tapped?"

"Probably not." Salvatore shook his head. "And even if it is, the penthouse is equipped with devices that scramble your signal. However, that doesn't stop listening devices on the other end. We can use that to our advantage, though, by scripting what you say."

"This is insane." She pressed a trembling hand to her forehead.

"I agree." Salvatore played the conciliatory role well, one he sure as hell hadn't shown a bunch of screwed-up teenagers seventeen years ago. "I sincerely hope we're wrong and all of this will be resolved quickly. But we can't afford to count on that. You need to tell them that you're ironing out details of the divorce with Conrad and it's taking longer than you expected."

Nodding, she stood, hitching her evening bag

over her shoulder. "I'll step into the kitchen, if that's not a problem."

"Take your time, catch your breath, but keep in mind we need to leave by sunup."

Jayne shot a quick glance at her husband, full of confusion, anger—betrayal—and then disappeared into the kitchen.

Conrad reined in his temper, lining up his thoughts and plans while his wife's soft voice drifted out.

Salvatore cleared his throat. "Do you have something to say, Hughes?"

Oh, he had plenty to say, but he needed to narrow his attention to the task at hand. "With all due respect, Colonel, it's best that I keep my opinions to myself and focus on how the hell we're going to keep Jayne off of that megalomaniac's radar."

"I have faith you'll handle that just fine."

The colonel's blasé answer lit the fuse to Conrad's anger. He closed the gap between them and hissed low between his teeth so Jayne wouldn't overhear. "If you have such faith in me, why the big show in front of my wife?"

"Big show?" He lifted an eyebrow.

What the hell? Conrad was not sixteen and a high school screwup. This was not the time for games. "Scaring the hell out of her. Springing the whole Interpol connection on her."

"I still can't believe you never told her. I thought you were smarter than that, my boy."

"It doesn't matter what you think. That was my call to make. I told you when I married her I didn't want her involved in that side of my life, for her own safety."

"Seems to me you've put her in more danger by not clueing her in. Even she picked up on that."

There was no way to know for sure now. But the possibility chapped at the worst time possible. "Thanks for the insights. Now, moving on to how we take care of Zhutov? If my cover's been compromised…"

The ramifications of that rolled over him, the realization that even once he had Jayne tucked away safe, this line of work and the redemption it brought could be closed to him forever. Later, he would sift through that and the possibility that without Interpol in his life, he could have his wife back.

Right now, he could only concentrate on making sure nobody touched so much as one hair on her head.

Sagging back against the polished pewter countertop, Jayne hugged her cell phone to her chest. The lies she'd just told left a bad taste in her mouth. Not to mention the fact she'd just been put on an unpaid leave of absence from her job.

This was supposed to have been such a simple trip to tie up the loose ends in her marriage…

Hell. Who was she kidding? Nothing with Conrad had ever been simple.

As if conjured from her thoughts, he filled the archway leading into the kitchen. He'd ditched his tuxedo jacket and tie, the top button of his shirt open. A light scratch marked his neck and

she realized she must have put it there some-
time during their grope fest in the elevator, along
with spiking his hair in her desperate hunger
to touch him again. Thank God she hadn't followed through. How much worse this moment
would have been had that elevator stayed shut
down and she'd made love with him standing up
in that cubicle of mirrors.

She set her phone down. "Can I have my panties back?"

He quirked an arrogant eyebrow before dip-
ping into his pocket and passing over the torn
scrap of satin. It was ridiculous really, asking for
the useless piece of underwear back, but it felt
like a statement of independence to her, reclaim-
ing ground and putting space between them.

She snatched the dangling white scrap from
his hand. "Thank you."

She jammed the underwear into the trash, a
minor victory, before turning back to confront
him. "You work for Interpol."

Hands in his pockets, he lounged one shoulder against the door frame. "Apparently I do."

Apparently?

His dodgy answer echoed too many in their past. The time he'd missed their first anniversary weekend retreat that they'd planned for weeks. Or when he'd bailed on going with her to her half brother's incredibly awkward wedding. And no explanations. Ever.

She couldn't keep quiet. Not now with her emotions still so raw from their explosive discussion in the car and their passionate encounter in the elevator. Even now, a need throbbed between her legs to finish what they'd started, to take him deeply inside her.

"You still won't admit it? Even when your boss confirmed it to me? What kind of twisted bastard are you? Do you get some sick pleasure out of yanking me around this way?"

His eyebrows shot up. "I kept you in the dark for your protection."

"I'm not buying it. I know you too well." Anger, hurt—and yes, more than a little sexual frustration—seethed inside her. "You didn't tell me because then you would have to commit, one hundred percent, to our marriage. You never wanted it to last, or you would have found a way to put my mind at ease all these years."

He could have told her something. Anything. But he hadn't even tried to come up with a rationale for his disappearances. He'd just *left*.

"I thought you would worry more," he said simply.

Although she wondered if there was a flash of guilt in his mocha-brown eyes. That would go a long way toward keeping her from pummeling him with fruit from the bowl on the counter.

"And you think I didn't worry when I had no clue where you were or what you were doing?" Those sleepless nights came back to haunt her. "In the beginning, I was scared to death something had happened to you those times I couldn't locate you. It took me a long time to reach the conclusion you must be cheating on me, like my father fooled around on my mom."

He straightened, his eyes flinty hard. "I never slept with another woman."

"I get that." She raised a hand. "Hell, I figured

that out even then. But you still lied to me. You cheated on me with that damn job."

He scrubbed a hand over his scowl. "Do you think operatives have the luxury of printing out an itinerary for their spouses?"

"Of course not. I'm not that naive." More like she'd let herself stay oblivious, clinging to the hope she might be wrong about him hiding things from her. "But Colonel Salvatore made it clear tonight you could have told me something and you chose not to."

"I chose what I thought was best for you." His mouth went tight.

Well, too damn bad. She had every right to be upset.

"You thought it was best to sacrifice our marriage? Because that's the decision you made for both of us, without even giving me the option of deciding for myself."

"I won't apologize for keeping you safe."

His intractable words made her realize how far apart they were from seeing eye to eye on this.

"Fine. But consider how you'd feel if the tables

were turned and it was me disappearing for days on end without a word of explanation. Or what you would have thought if I'd left you to celebrate your anniversary by yourself." He'd flown her to a couples retreat in the Seychelles. The island country off the coast of Africa had been so romantic and exotic. Except he'd left her sitting in a dining room full of hormones all alone.

He'd said nothing, as per usual.

Knowing she'd let herself be turned into some kind of doll adorning his arm and decorating his world perhaps stung most of all. "And to think I was that close to falling in your arms again. Well, no worries about that now. I am so over you, Conrad Hughes."

She angled sideways past him, through the door.

He gripped her arm. "You can't leave now. No matter how angry you are with me, it's not safe for you out there."

"I got that from your boss, thanks. I'm just going to pack. In my room. *Alone*."

His hand slid down her arm, sending a traitorous jolt of awareness straight to her belly until she pressed her legs together against the moist ache still simmering.

"You were able to arrange things with work and for Mimi?"

Standing this close to Conrad with her emotions on overload was not a smart idea. She needed to wrap this up and retreat to her room to regroup. "She's settled, but Anthony can't watch her indefinitely. He travels with his job. But I'll figure that out later."

She brushed past.

"Anthony."

Conrad's flat, emotionless voice sent prickles up her spine. She turned slowly, her evening gown brushing the tops of her bare feet. "He's the nephew of a former patient."

Not that she owed him any explanation after the way he'd walled her out for years.

"And he watches our dog while you're out of town." Conrad still leaned in the doorway, completely motionless other than the slow blink of his too-sharp eyes.

"It's not like he and I are dating…"

"Yet. But that's why you came to Monte Carlo, isn't it? So you would be free to move on with Anthony or some other guy." Conrad scratched his eyebrow. "I think I pretty much have the picture in place."

And clearly he wasn't one bit happy with that image. Well, too damn bad after all the tears she'd shed seeing his casino pictured in tabloids, him with a different woman on his arm each time. "You don't get to be mad at me. I'm the one who's been lied to."

"Then I guess that makes it easier for us to spend time alone together." He shoved away from the door frame, his shoulder brushing hers as he passed. "Pack your bag, sweetheart. We're taking a family vacation."

Six

The bulletproof, tinted windows on his balcony offered Conrad the protection he needed while escaping the claustrophobic air of the penthouse.

Jayne had already picked out his replacement. He realized now that she'd come to Monte Carlo to end their marriage so she could move on with another man. If she hadn't already.

Scratch that.

He didn't think she was sleeping with the guy, not yet. Jayne was an innately honorable woman. And while he didn't assume she would stay celibate for three years, she wouldn't have almost had sex with him if she'd already committed to another man.

Her integrity was one of the things about her that had drawn him right from the start. She had a goodness inside her that was rare and should be protected. For the first time, it hit him how much she must have missed her career when she lived with him, and even though Monte Carlo was his primary residence, he'd traveled from holding to holding too often for her to secure a new job. He'd never thought about how long and lonely her days must have been.

Looking back, he probably should have left her the hell alone. He deserved Jayne's anger and more. He'd been wrong to marry her in the first place knowing he would never choose to tell her about his contract work with Interpol. He'd deluded himself that he held back out of a need to protect her, but deep down he knew he'd always feared he needed the job more than he needed her. That he needed that outlet to rebel, a way to channel the part of his father that lived inside him, the part that had almost landed him in jail as a teenager.

He'd been so damn crazy for Jayne he'd convinced himself he could make it work.

He'd only delayed the inevitable.

Now she was paying the price for his mistake. He resisted the urge to put his fist through a wall. Her life could be at risk because of him. He wouldn't be able to live with himself if anything happened to her.

He scoured the cove below, every yacht and cruise ship lighting up the shoreline suddenly became suspect.

A sound from the doorway sent him pivoting fast, his hand on the 9mm he'd strapped into a shoulder harness.

Troy Donavan lounged in the entrance, his fedora in hand. "Whoa, hold up. Don't shoot your body double."

"My what?"

Donavan stepped out onto the balcony. "Your double. I'll travel as you and you travel as me. If anyone manages to track either of our move-

ments, they'll still be led in the wrong direction."
He dropped his hat on the lounger. "Salvatore
said we're not heading out for another couple of
hours. I can keep watch over Jayne while you
catch a nap."

"I'm cool. But thanks. Insomnia has its perks."
He glanced sideways at his best friend of over
seventeen years. "Did Salvatore send you here to
check on me after the showdown with Jayne?"

"He alerted me to the crap with Zhutov and
the concerns for your wife. I know how I would
feel in your shoes, and it's not pretty."

Damn straight. He didn't know how Donavan
handled having Hillary keyed into the Interpol
world. She'd even started training to actively
participate in future freelance missions.

"I have to get Jayne as far away and under the
radar as possible." How long would this nightmare last? Would she end up spending the rest
of her life on the run? He wouldn't leave her
side until he knew she was safe. He'd wanted to
grow old with her, but sure as hell not that way.

"I promise you, brother, if Zhutov has so much

as breathed Jayne's name, he will be stopped. You have to believe that."

"After this is over, I have to let her go." Those words were tough to say, especially now with the image of her building a life with another man. "I was wrong to think I could have her and the job."

"People do dangerous jobs and still have lives. You can't expect every cop, firefighter, military person and agent not to have families. Even if we don't get married, there are still people in our lives who are important to us. The best thing you can do for Jayne is stick to her, tight."

"You're right."

"Then why aren't you smiling?" Donavan clapped him on the shoulder. "Want to talk about what else is chewing you up?"

"Not really."

"Fair enough."

And still he couldn't stop from talking. "She just…gets to me."

He remembered the way she'd called him on the carpet for teasing her on the ride home tonight, giving him hell for talking about that evening they saw *La Bohème* together. As if he knew that would turn her inside out the same way it did him. Damn, he'd missed that spark she possessed.

"That's what women do. They burrow under your skin." Donavan grinned. "Didn't you get the memo?"

Conrad didn't feel one damn bit like smiling. He stared down at his clenched fist, at his own bare ring finger. "She's seeing someone else."

"Damn," Donavan growled. "That's got to really bite. But it's been three years since the two of you split. Did you really expect you would both stay celibate?"

Conrad looked out over the harbor, the sea stretching as far and dark as each day he'd spent apart from Jayne.

Troy straightened quickly. "Whoa, wait. Are you telling me you haven't seen anyone else while you've been separated?"

Still, Conrad held his silence.

"But the tabloids…"

"They lie." Conrad smiled wryly at his friend. "Didn't you get the memo?"

Donavan stared back, not even bothering to disguise his total shock. "You haven't been with anybody in *three years?*"

"I'm married." He thumbed his empty ring finger. "A married man does not cheat. It's dishonorable."

Donavan scrubbed both hands over his face then shook his head as if to clear the shock away. "So let me get this straight… You haven't seen your wife since she left you. Which means you haven't had sex with anyone in *three years?*"

"You're a damn genius."

Donavan whistled softly. "You must be having some serious quality 'alone time' in the shower."

Understatement of the year. Or rather, that would be *three* years. "Your sympathy for my pain is overwhelming."

"Doesn't sound like you need sympathy. Sounds like you need to get—"

"Thanks," he interrupted, not even wanting

to risk Donavan's words putting images in his head. "I can handle my own life."

"Because you're doing such a bang-up job at it lately. But wait." He thumped himself on the forehead. "Poor choice of words."

Against his will, a smile tugged at Conrad's face. "Really, Donovan. Don't you have some geeky computer tech support work that needs your attention before we all leave?"

"You can call me a geek all night long, brother, but I'll be sleeping next to a woman." Donavan punched him in the arm.

Conrad lifted an eyebrow, but preferred the joking to sympathy any day of the week. Something his best friend undoubtedly understood. "Hit me again, and I'm going to beat the crap out of you."

Donavan snagged his fedora from the lounger. "Everybody wants to beat the crap out of me today. What's up with that?"

"Get out of here before I break you in half."

"Because I feel very sorry for you, I'm just going to walk away." He spun his hat on one finger. "But I'm taking a bottle of your Chivas with me so you won't feel bad for scaring me off."

"Jackass."

"I feel the love, brother. I feel the love." He opened the French doors and paused, half in, half out. "See you inside later?"

"Absolutely." He nodded once. "And thank you."

Donavan nodded back. No more words were needed.

His friend had helped him decompress enough to see clearly again. He needed to keep his eye on the goal now, to keep Jayne safe at all cost.

He might not be the man she deserved, but he was damn well the man she needed.

Jayne rolled her small bag out into the living room, having used the past couple of hours to change out of her evening gown and generally get her head together. If that was even possible after her world had been so deeply shaken in such a short time.

The sun hadn't even risen yet.

If they hadn't been interrupted, she would have been in Conrad's bed now, completely unsuspecting of *this*.

She realized his secret had noble roots, a profession that brought justice, so different than her father's secret life, his hidden second family with a mistress and two children. But the fact that she'd been duped so totally still hurt on a deep level. Trusting her heart and her life to Conrad had been very difficult.

How could she reconcile the fact that she hadn't even begun to know the man she'd married? Walking away with any kind of peace when she'd thought she understood him was tough enough. But now with so much mystery surrounding Conrad and their life together, she felt like every bit of progress she'd made since leaving had been upended.

And with this possible threat lurking, she didn't even have the luxury of distance to regain her footing.

The Donavans sat in the leather chairs, talking over glasses of seltzer water. She felt uncomfortable having Troy and Hillary pose as decoys for them. The thought of anybody in harm's way because of her made her ill. But she hadn't been given any say on the matter.

She also couldn't help but note how seamlessly Hillary had been brought into the plan. Apparently not all Interpol operatives kept secrets from their spouses.

The stab of envy for that kind of compatibility wasn't something she was proud of. But, damn it, why couldn't she have found her way to that sort of comfort with her husband? What was wrong with her that Conrad had never even considered confiding in her?

Just as she rolled her bag the rest of the way in, Conrad stepped out of his suite. His normal dark and brooding style of clothes had been swapped out for something more in keeping with Troy's metro style. She couldn't take her eyes from the relaxed look of her husband in jeans and a jacket, collar open, face unshaved, his thick black hair spiked.

Troy looked back over the chair, water glass in

hand. "Good timing. Salvatore should be done any minute now. He's arranging the travel plans, complete with diversionary stories going out to the press." He glanced over at his wife. "Did I forget anything?"

"Just this." Carrying one of her husband's hats, Hillary walked to Conrad. "You should wear this. And maybe slick back your hair a bit. Here…" She reached for her water glass. "Use some of this since you didn't have time to shower."

Troy choked on his drink.

Conrad glared at him.

Jayne wondered what in the world was wrong with both of them.

Her husband took the fedora from Hillary. "I'm good. Thanks. I'll take good care of his hat."

"Take good care of yourself while you're at it," Hillary said just as her husband looped an arm around her waist and hauled her to his side. "Yes?"

Troy held up his phone. "Text from Salvatore. Time to roll."

With a hurried goodbye, Troy and Hillary stepped into the elevator, his head bent toward hers to listen to something. The two of them looked so right together, so in sync even in the middle of chaos.

Jealousy gripped Jayne in an unrelenting fist.

The doors slid closed and she wished her feelings could be as easily sealed away. She turned back to her husband. "Where are we going?"

Conrad thumbed through his text message, Troy's fedora under his arm. "To the jet."

"And the jet would be going to…"

He looked up, his eyes piercing and closed off all at once. "Somewhere far away from here."

His evasive answer set her teeth on edge. "Now that I know about your double life, you can drop the tall, dark and mysterious act."

She yanked the fedora from under his arm, his jacket parting.

A shoulder holster held a silver handgun.

"Oh," she gasped, knowing she shouldn't be surprised, but still just… "Oh."

He pulled his jacket back over the weapon.

"The people I help nail don't play nice. They are seriously dangerous. You can be as angry at me as you want, but you'll have to trust me, just this once, and save your questions for the airplane. I promise I'll tell you anything you want to know once we're airborne. Agreed?"

Anything she wanted to know? That was one promise she couldn't resist. Probably the very reason he'd said it, tossing irresistible temptation her way. But it was an offer she intended to press to the fullest.

She pulled out a silk scarf to wrap over her blond hair. "Lead the way."

Once the chartered jet reached cruising altitude, Conrad took his first easy breath since he'd found Salvatore waiting for him in the penthouse. He was that much closer to having Jayne tucked away in the last place anyone would think to find either of them.

Jayne hadn't moved her eyes off him since they'd left the penthouse. Even now she sat on the other side of the small table, tugging her silk scarf from hand to hand. He watched the glide of the deep purple fabric as it slid from side to side. Until now, he hadn't realized she dressed in bolder colors these days. A simple thing and inconsequential, but yet another sign that she'd moved on since leaving him. She'd changed and he couldn't go back to the way things were.

But back to the moment. Without a doubt, the boom was going to fall soon and he would have to answer her questions. He owed her that much and more. He reached for his coffee on the small table between them, a light breakfast set in front of them.

He wasn't interested in food. Only Jayne. He could read her well and the second she set aside the scarf in her hands he knew. She was ready to talk.

"We're airborne, and you owe me answers." She drizzled honey into her tea. "Tell me where we're going."

"Africa."

Freezing midsip, she stared at him over the top of her cup. "Just when I think you can't surprise me. Are we staying somewhere like the island resort where we planned to spend our first anniversary?"

"No." He couldn't miss the subtle reminder of when he'd bailed on their first anniversary retreat in Seychelles. Without a doubt, he owed her for all the times he'd shortchanged her in the past. He raised the window shade, the first morning rays streaking through the clouds. "We're going to West Africa. I have a house there."

"Another thing I didn't know about you." Her voice dripped with frustration as thick as the extra honey she spooned into her tea. "Do you mean something like a safari resort?"

"Something like that, nothing to do with business, though." She would see for herself soon enough, and he had to admit, he wanted to see her reaction without prior warning. "I purchased the property just before we split. A case led me to… It doesn't matter. You're right. I should have told you about an acquisition that large."

"If it's your home, can't we be found there?"

"The property was purchased under a corporate name, nothing anyone would connect with me. There's not much point in a retreat if the paparazzi can find you."

"Well, if the press hasn't found out about it, then the place must be secure." She half smiled. "So do we plan to hide in Africa indefinitely?"

"What did you tell Anthony?" He set down his coffee cup carefully.

"It's my turn to ask the questions, remember?" she reminded him gently. Her eyes fell away, and she stared into her cup as if searching for answers of her own. "But in the interest of peace… I told him what we planned for me to say, that divorcing my husband wasn't as simple as I'd expected. That you and I needed time to sort things out. He was understanding."

"Then he isn't as big a threat as I thought." He couldn't wrap his brain around the notion of ever being okay with the prospect of Jayne and some other guy hooking up. His hand twitched around the cup.

"Conrad, not everyone is all alpha, all the time."

He looked up fast, surprised at her word choice then chuckled.

"What did I say? And remember, you promised to answer my questions."

At least he could tell her this and wondered now why he never had before. "Back in high school, my friends, we called ourselves the Alpha Brotherhood."

"You're all still so close." She frowned. "Do they *all* work for…"

"Please don't ask."

"You said I could ask anything," she pressed stubbornly.

He searched for what he could say and still stay honest. "If something were to happen to me and you needed anything at all, you could call them. They can get in touch with Salvatore. Is that answer enough for you?"

She stared at him for so long he thought she might push for more, and truly there was more he could say but old instincts died hard after playing his life close to the vest.

Nodding, she leaned back in her leather seat,

crossing her arms. "Thank you. Get back to the Alpha Brotherhood story."

"There were two kinds of guys at the academy, the military sort who wanted to be there to jump-start a career in uniform and a bunch of screwed-up rule breakers who needed to learn discipline."

Did she know that when she'd leaned back her legs stretched out in a sexy length that made him ache? He wanted to reach down and stroke her calf, so close to touching him. The sight of her in those jeans and leather boots sent another shot of adrenaline to his already overrevved body.

He knocked back another swallow of hot coffee to moisten his suddenly dry mouth. "Some of us in that second half realized the wisdom of channeling those rebellious tendencies if we wanted to stay out of jail. After we graduated from college, Salvatore offered us a legal outlet, a way to make amends and still color outside the lines—legally. Honorably."

"That's important to you, honor." She crossed her legs at the ankles, bringing her booted foot even closer to brushing him. "You've been so emphatic about never lying even when you hold back the truth."

He looked up sharply, realizing how much he'd revealed while ogling her legs like some horny teenager. And he realized she was playing him. Just like he'd played her in the past, using sexual attraction to steer their conversations.

It didn't feel good being maneuvered that way.

Remorse took his temperature down a notch. He sat up straighter, elbows on the table as he cradled his coffee. "My father was a crooked bastard, Jayne. It makes me sick the way the rest of the world all thought he was this great philanthropist. He made a crap-ton of money and gave it away to charities. But he made it cheating the same kinds of people he was pretending to help."

Her hand fell to rest on his. "I understand what it's like to lose faith in your father. It hurts, so much."

How strange that he was holding hands with his wife and he couldn't remember the last time he'd done that. He'd touched her, stroked her, made love to her countless times, but he couldn't recall holding her hand.

"I guess we do have that in common. For a long time, I bought into my old man's hype. I thought he was some kind of god."

"You've never told me how your mother felt about your father's crimes?"

"She's his accountant." He shrugged, thinking of all the times he got an attaboy from his parents for making the grade. It never mattered how, as long as he won. "Colonel Salvatore was the first person to ever hold my feet to the fire about anything. Yes, I have my own code of honor now, Jayne. I have to be able to look myself in the mirror, and this job is the only way I know how to make that happen."

"How weird is it that we've been married for seven years and there are still so many things about you I don't know." Her blue eyes held him as tangibly as her hand held his beside the plate of croissants and éclairs.

"That's my fault." He squeezed.

"Damn straight it is." She squeezed back.

The jet engine droned in the silence between them, recycled air whooshing down.

He flipped her hand in his and stroked her lifeline with his thumb. "What happens now?"

"What do you mean?" Her voice came out breathy, her chest rising and falling faster.

Although he could see that even in her anger she still wanted him, he was now beginning to understand that desire alone wouldn't cut it any longer.

"In the elevator we were a zipper away from making love again."

Her hand went still in his, her eyes filled with a mix of desire and frustration. "And you want to pick up where we left off?"

"How will your dog sitter feel about that?"

She sighed. "Are you still jealous even after I told you I'm not dating him?"

"Are you planning on seeing him after you leave?" He had to know, even if the answer skewered him.

What had the other guy given her that he couldn't? He'd lavished her with every single thing a woman could want, and it hadn't been enough for Jayne.

"Honestly," she said, "I thought I might when I flew to Monte Carlo, but now, I'm not sure anymore."

He started to reach for her but she stopped him cold with a tight shake of her head.

"Damn it, Jayne—"

"I'm not done." She squeezed his hand hard. "Don't take what I said as some sign to start tearing our clothes off. I *am* certain that I want a normal life with a husband who will be there for me. I want the happily ever after with kids and a real family sitting down to dinner together, even if it's hamburgers on a rickety picnic table at a simple hometown park. Maybe that sounds boring to you, but I just can't pretend to fit into this jet-set lifestyle of yours where we share a bed and nothing else. Does that make sense?"

He closed his eyes, only to be blindsided by the image of her sitting on a porch swing with some other lucky bastard while their kids played in the yard. "The thought of you with someone else is chewing me up inside."

"You don't have the right to ask anymore," she said gently. "You know that, don't you? We've been separated for three years."

"Tell that to my chewed-up gut."

She tugged her hand free. "You've already moved on. Why shouldn't I?"

He looked up sharply. "Says who?"

"Every tabloid in the stands."

"Tabloids. Really?" He laughed. Hard. Not that it made him feel any better. "That's where you're getting your news from? I thought you graduated from college magna cum laude."

Finally he'd shocked her quiet, silencing those damn probing questions.

But not for long.

Jayne's hand clenched around her discarded scarf. "You're saying it's not true? That you haven't been with other women since we split up?"

He leaned across the table until his mouth was barely an inch away from hers. He could feel her breath on his skin and he knew she felt his. Her pupils widened in awareness, sensual anticipation. And still, he held back. He wouldn't kiss her now, not this way, when he was still so angry his vision clouded.

Not to mention his judgment.

He looked her in the eyes and simply said, "I am a married man. I take that commitment very seriously."

She was his wife. The only woman he'd ever loved. He should have the answers locked and loaded on how to keep her happy. He was a damn Wall Street genius, entrepreneur billionaire and Interpol agent, for God's sake.

Yet right now, he didn't have a clue how to make things right with Jayne, and he didn't know if he ever would.

Seven

The gates swung wide to Conrad's home in Africa, and Jayne had to admit, he'd shocked the hell out of her twice in less than twenty-four hours.

She'd expected a grand mansion, behind massive walls with sleek security systems that made Batman's cave look like something from last generation's game system. This place was…

Understated.

And the quiet beauty of it took her breath away.

She leaned forward in the seat, as the Land Cruiser took the uphill dirt road. A ranch-style house perched on a natural plateau overlooking

a river. She'd spent four years poring over reno-
vations and perfect pieces of furniture for their
different residences, perhaps hoping she could
somehow create an ideal marriage if she could
only put together an ideal home. She would
guess the place was built from authentic African walnut. Everything about the house looked
real, nothing prefab or touristy about it.

Porches—and more porches—wrapped around
the lengthy wooden home, with rockers, tables
and roll down screens to overlook the nearby
river. Palm trees had a more tropical than land-
scaped feel. Mangrove trees reached for the sky
with their gnarled roots twisting up from the
ground like wads of fat cables.

She glanced at her husband, wondering what
led him to purchase this place just before they'd
split. But his stoic face wasn't giving away any
clues. Although, Lord, have mercy, he was as
magnificent as the stark and unforgiving landscape.

With the day heating up fast, he'd ditched the
sports coat and just wore jeans with his shirt-

sleeves rolled up. Like his home, he didn't need extravagant trappings to take her breath away. As if she wasn't already tempted enough around him.

Although the gun still tucked in the shoulder harness gave her more than a little pause.

Their game of twenty questions during the plane ride hadn't helped her understand him one bit better. If anything, she had more questions, more reservations. Being here alone together was complicated now. They'd moved past the idea of sex for the hell of it as some farewell tribute to their marriage. That didn't mean the attraction wasn't still there, fierce as ever, just beneath the surface of their tentative relationship.

Tearing her gaze away, she pressed her hands to the dash. "This isn't at all what I expected."

"How so?" He slowed the SUV then stopped at the half-dozen wooden steps leading to the front door.

"No bells and whistles chiming. No gambling rich and famous everywhere you look."

"The quiet appeals to me." He opened the door and circled the hood to her side.

She stepped out just as he reached her and avoided his outstretched hand, not ready to touch him again, not yet. "If you'd wanted somewhere to be quiet, there were places a lot closer to home than Africa."

The dusty wind tore at her hair. She tugged her scarf from around her neck and tied back the tangled mess.

"True. But this is the one I wanted and since I'm sinfully rich," he said, pulling out her roll bag and a duffel for himself, "I can have the things I want, if not the people."

Was this quieter persona one he donned for his missions or was this a part of her husband she'd never seen? She shivered in spite of the temps already sending a trickle of sweat down her spine. "What about security? I don't see any fences or cameras."

"Of course you didn't see them as we drove up. They're the best, thanks to our good friend Troy. If anyone crosses the perimeter, we'll know." He jogged up the stairs and flipped back a shutter to reveal an electronics panel. "You'll be briefed on how everything works so you're not dependent on me if an emergency arises."

Now wasn't that an eye opener?

She trailed her fingers along a rocker, setting it in motion and thought of his casino with the glassed-in balcony overlooking the sea. And she realized he loved the outdoors. Even now, his ear tipped toward the monkey chattering from some hidden tree branch.

"Jayne?" he called from the open door. "Are you ready?"

"Of course," she lied and followed him inside anyway.

This was definitely not a safari lodge after all.

There weren't any animal heads mounted on the walls, just paintings, an amalgamation of watercolors, oils and charcoals, without a defining theme other than the fact each one portrayed a unique view of Africa.

And in such a surprisingly open space.

Conrad had a style of his own—and a damn

good one. But she'd fallen into a stereotypical assumption that he would put a foosball table in her living room if she turned over the reins to him. She thought back to his penthouse remodeling. She'd been so focused on the shock of all her things swept away she'd failed to notice the sense of style even in his man cave.

How much of his "hiding" of himself had she let happen?

She stepped deeper into the room with a massive stone fireplace in the middle. A wood frame sectional sofa dominated the space, piled with natural fiber cushions and pillows. There were no distractions here, just the echo of her footsteps and the sound of the breeze rustling branches outdoors.

The place was larger on the inside than it looked from outdoors, likely another means of security. Her entire condo back in Miami could have fit in the living area with room to spare. A glance down the hall showed at least five other doors, but she was drawn to the window overlooking the river. A small herd of antelope waded in for a drink, while a hippo lazed on the far side of the shore.

Conrad's hand fell on her shoulder. "Jayne?"

She jolted and spun to face him, finding him so close her heart leaped into her throat. Her hands started to press to his chest, but she stopped shy of the silver gun.

"Uh, I was just enjoying the view." She gestured over her shoulder at the window.

"You've been standing there awhile. I thought you'd dozed off." He tugged the end of her scarf, her hair sliding loose again. "You must be almost dead on your feet since we didn't sleep last night, so I'll save the grand tour for later. There's just one place you need to see now."

The kitchen for a snack? His bed to make love before they both fell into an exhausted slumber?

He stopped in front of a Picasso-style watercolor of people in bright colors dancing. He slid the painting to the side to reveal another panel like the one she'd seen on the front door. After a quick tap along the keypad, he stepped back.

Boards along the wall slid automatically and stacked, revealing a passage.

"This is the panic room." Conrad pressed a card into her hand with a series of numbers. "This is the code. Do not hesitate to use it in case of an emergency. Don't wait for me. I can take care of myself a helluva lot better if I'm not worrying about you."

Salvatore's words from earlier came back to haunt her, about how she was Conrad's Achilles' heel. Her presence placed him in greater danger. Somehow in the rush to leave Monte Carlo, she'd lost sight of that revelation.

Tears burned her eyes, and she ached to reach for him.

"Jayne, it's going to be okay." He brushed her hair over her shoulder. "You need to sleep, and I need to check the place over. We'll talk more later."

She tried not to feel rebuffed. He was doing his job. *She* had pushed *him* away after Salvatore's revelation.

Her hands fell to her sides. Of course he was

right. She couldn't possibly make rational deci-
sions with her head cottony from lack of sleep.
And if she couldn't think clearly she became
even more of a liability to Conrad.

Yet as he showed her to the guest room, she
still couldn't help wishing she could sleep in his
arms.

Conrad punched in the code to the safe room
where he stored all his communication gear and
security equipment. The entire place ran off
solar power and a satellite feed, so he couldn't be
cut off from the outside world. He kept enough
water and nonperishable food in storage to out-
last a siege.

Call him paranoid, but even in his infrequent
freelance role with Interpol, he'd seen some intense crap go down in the world.

The windowless vault room in the middle of
the house had everything he needed—a bed,
an efficiency kitchen, a bathroom and a sitting
area, small, but useful down to the last detail. A
flat screen was mounted on the wall for watch-

ing the exterior. And an entire office's worth of computers were stored away, ready to fold out onto the dinette table like an ironing board lowered out of a wall.

He parked himself in front of the secured laptop and reached for the satellite phone. He needed to check in with Salvatore. Halfway through the first ring, his boss answered.

"Yes," the colonel barked.

"We've arrived, and we're settled. No red flags here that I can see. What do you have on your end?"

"The money in Zhutov's wife's account has been withdrawn and we have images—which I'm forwarding to you now—of his known associates in discussion with a hit man. We've got trackers on both individuals."

"I'll review his wife's bank accounts again. Why her assets haven't been frozen is beyond me."

"We do what we can, and you know that."

"Well, let's damn well do more." Scrolling through computer logs of account transfers,

Conrad tucked the phone between his shoulder and ear, not wanting to risk speakerphone where Jayne might wake up and overhear.

"Hughes, my people are on it. You should sleep. You'll be more alert."

"Like you sleep?"

The colonel was a well-known workaholic. When they'd all been in school they'd theorized that their headmaster was a robot who didn't need mere mortal things like sleep. Seemed as if he was always walking the halls, day and night.

Salvatore sighed. "Go spend some time with your wife. Repair you marriage. Put your life back together again."

"Sir, with all due respect, you saw her back in Monte Carlo. She was pissed."

"I saw a woman who looked like she'd just been kissed senseless in an elevator."

"You're not helping the problem at hand by playing matchmaker." He'd need more of a miracle worker to untangle the mess he'd made of his life.

"I sincerely hope you and she had a long talk on the airplane about your work with me."

Just what he needed right now, a damn lecture on all the ways he'd screwed up his marriage. "Thank you for your input, sir. I'll take that under advisement."

The colonel laughed darkly. "Still as stubborn as ever, Hughes. Leave the sleuthing to my end this time. Your job is to fly under the radar, keep you and your wife safe. Let me know if you need anything."

The call disconnected, and Conrad set the phone aside.

Three fruitless hours of database searching later, he slammed the computer shut in frustration. He couldn't figure out if the clues just weren't there. Salvatore's words echoed through his head, about his job being to protect Jayne. The old colonel was right. Conrad wouldn't be any good to her dead on his feet.

Resigned to surrendering, at least for now, he left the panic room and sealed it up tight again. The sectional sofa looked about as inviting as a bed of nails, but it was the best place to keep an ear out for Jayne—other than sleeping next to her, which didn't appear to be an option tonight.

And speaking of Jayne, he needed to check on her, to leave her door open a crack so he could hear her even in his sleep. He padded barefoot down the hall to her room and eased her door open.

Bad idea.

Looking at Jayne sleeping was torture. And apparently he was a masochist tonight because he stepped deeper into her room. Her legs were tangled in the sheets, long legs bared since her nightgown had hitched up. Her silky hair splashed over the pillow in a feathery blond curtain.

She slept curled on her side, with a pillow hugged to her chest just the way he remembered. If they'd still been together, he would have curled up behind her, their bodies a perfect fit. He still didn't understand how something so incredibly good could fall apart like their marriage had.

Tired of torturing himself tonight, he pivoted

away and walked back out to the living room. He yanked a blanket off the ladder rack against the wall and grabbed two throw pillows. Even if his mind resisted shutting down, his body demanded that he stretch out and rest. But still his brain churned with thoughts of Jayne and how damn close they'd been to making love again.

If Salvatore hadn't been waiting for them in the penthouse, they would have ended up in bed. He could still hear her cries of pleasure from the elevator. He could feel the silken texture of her clamping around his fingers.

They may have had their problems communicating, but when it came to sex, they'd always been beyond compatible. And they'd had other things in common, too, damn it. They shared similar taste in books and politics. She enjoyed travel and appreciated the beauty of a sunset anywhere in the world.

And they both enjoyed the opera.

In fact, he'd planned to take her to the opera during their forty-eight hours of romance, back when he'd been enough of an idiot to think he could let her go again. He'd chartered a jet to fly them to Venice for a performance. He'd reserved a plush, private opera box where he could replay their *La Bohème* date.

He could still remember what she wore that night, a pale blue gown, feathery light. He'd been riding the rush of a recent mission, adrenaline making him ache all the more for his wife. The moment he'd seen her walk out of their bedroom wearing the dress, he'd known he wouldn't rest until he found out what she had on underneath.

Before Act One was complete, he'd known....

Dreams of Conrad during that hazy realm of twilight sleep always tormented her the most. Fantasy and reality blended until she didn't know whether to force herself awake or cling to sleep longer.

La Bohème echoed through her mind, the opening act, except that didn't make sense because she was in Africa with Conrad. So why was the opera playing out on a barge on the river? Confusion threatened to pull her awake. Until the glide of Conrad's hands over her breasts made her cling to the dream realm where she could sit with her husband on the porch and listen.

Savor.

His hands slid down her stomach to her leg. With skillful fingers he bunched her gauzy blue evening gown up, up, up her leg until his hand tunneled underneath. She felt his frown and realized she had jeans on underneath her formal dress?

Confusion churned in her brain as she stared down at her bare feet and well-worn denim. She kicked at the hem of her gown, frustrated, needing to free herself of the voluminous folds so she could wear her jeans.

And so she could feel Conrad's touch.

The roar of frustration grew louder, and louder still until the porch disintegrated from the vibrations. She stood in the rubble, a herd of elephants kicking up dust on the horizon.

Her bare feet pedaled against the covers. She fought harder, frantic to wake herself up and outrun the beasts chasing through her head.

Elephants thundered behind her, rumbling the ground along with an orchestra segueing into the closing act. Her chest hurt, and she gasped for air.

She tripped over the gnarled roots of a mango tree. Her hands slapped the ground, but it gave way, plunging her into the Mediterranean Sea outside Conrad's casino. The farther she sank, the darker the waters became until she hit bottom.

Sealed in a panic room.

A window cleared along the top and she looked up, searching for a way out. Desperation squeezed the air from her lungs. Conrad stood on the balcony far, far above, watching her, drinking his Chivas. She couldn't reach him, and he couldn't hear her choked cries of warning to watch out for the thundering herd.

Wasn't a guy always supposed to hear his mermaid call him?

Except she wasn't the one in danger.

His balcony filled with thick, noxious smoke until Conrad disappeared…

Jayne sat up sharply.

Wide-awake, she blinked in the dark, unfamiliar room. Gauzy mosquito netting trailed from all four corners of the canopy. Just a dream, she reminded herself. Not real.

Well, the charging elephants weren't real, but the panic room was very real, along with a looming threat.

Fear for Conrad still covered her like a thick blanket on a muggy day. She'd put him in danger just by being with him. A crummy way to pay him back for all the years he'd tried to keep her safe from a dangerous job. Now that she was past some of the worst feelings of betrayal, she could feel the inevitable admiration beneath it. He was a good man, and she—unknowingly—had been his Achilles' heel.

That hurt her to think about. She had so many regrets about her marriage, and their future had never been more complicated. Her body burned for his touch.

With the pain of losing him still so fresh in her mind, she knew without question, she *had* to be with him tonight.

* * *

Conrad stared at the ceiling fan swirling around and around, the click so quiet he knew that couldn't have woken him.

So what had?

The alarms were set. He'd cracked the door to Jayne's room. No one would get in without him knowing, and Jayne wouldn't so much as sneeze without him hearing.

Muffled cries? He'd absolutely heard those.

Hand on his 9mm, he raced down the hall, careful to keep his steps quiet so as not to alert an intruder. He pushed through the guest bedroom door.

And found Jayne standing a hand's reach away in an otherwise empty room. She jumped back to avoid the swinging door. The sight of her hit him clean in the libido.

His hand fell away from his gun.

An icy-blue nightgown stopped just shy of her knees, lace trim teasing creamy flesh. The pale blue was so close to the color of the gown she'd worn to *La Bohème* that memorable night it almost knocked his feet out from under him. The silk clung to her curves the way his hands ached to do, the way he'd dreamed of doing every night since she'd walked out on him.

"Is something wrong? I heard you cry out in your sleep and I just needed to be sure you're all right." Good enough cover story for why he'd burst into the room.

"Just a nightmare. How cliché, huh?" She thrust her hands in her hair, pushing it back—and stretching the fabric of her nightgown across her breasts. "I cry out. You run to me in my bedroom, afraid something happened to me. I'm still rattled by my bad dream."

He tore his eyes off the pebbly tightness of her nipples against silk. "God forbid we should ever be cliché."

She stepped closer, padding slowly on bare feet, her eyes narrowed with a sensual intent he'd seen—and enjoyed—many times in the past.

"Although, Conrad, clichés become clichés because they worked well for a lot of other people. And if we follow the dream cliché to its conclusion, the next step would be for me to throw myself in your arms so we can make love."

Jayne stopped toe-to-toe with him, still not touching him, and if she did, his control would be shot all to hell. For whatever reason, she was taking charge and seducing him. Except she would be doing so for all the wrong reasons, vulnerable from whatever had frightened her in the dream.

He couldn't take advantage of her while she was riding the memories of a nightmare. But he also couldn't leave her in here upset and alone.

Grabbing the door to keep from reaching for her, he stepped back into the hall. "I think we need to get out of this bedroom."

"Why?" She nibbled her bottom lip.

He swallowed hard. "We need to go. Trust me."

She laughed softly. "Trust you? That's rich, coming from you."

"Fair enough, I deserve that." He always had liked the way she never pulled punches and found it every bit as arousing now as he had when they lived together. "Or you could just trust me because you're a nicer person than I am."

"All right, then." She placed her hand in his, her soft fingers curling around his.

And holy crap, she leaned in closer to him as they walked down the hall. The light scent of her shampoo teased his nose. The need to haul her into his arms throbbed harder, hotter. Damn it, he was supposed to be protecting her, comforting her. He reined in thoughts fueled by three years of abstinence.

Three. Damn. Years.

Out in the main living area, he guided her to the sectional sofa, wide palm ceiling fans clicking overhead. "Have a seat, and I'll get us a snack from the kitchen."

She settled onto the sofa, nestling in a pile of pillows. "Just some water, please."

That would give him all of sixty seconds to will back the raging erection. Hell, he could spend an hour creating a five course meal and it wouldn't be enough time to ease the painful arousal.

He snagged two bottles of water from the stainless-steel refrigerator in a kitchen he'd actually learned to use and returned to the living room. He twisted off a cap and passed her the Evian. "Let's watch a movie."

"A movie?"

"I can pipe anything you want in through the satellite." He opened his bottle. "I'm even open to a chick flick."

"You want to watch a *movie?*" She shifted in the mass of throw pillows, looking so much like a harem girl he almost dropped to his knees.

"Or we can talk." And he realized now that Salvatore was right. He should talk to Jayne and tell her more about the man she'd married, the man she thought she wanted to crawl back in bed with. He needed to be sure her eyes were wide-open about him before he could even consider taking her up on what she offered.

She was stuck here because of him. They were both forced to watch over their shoulders—also because of him and the choices he'd made. While he couldn't see much he would do differently, at least he owed her a better perspective on why he'd broken the law.

Why he'd ruined so many lives, including theirs.

He sat by her, on the side that didn't have his gun in the way. On second thought, he un-strapped the shoulder harness and set the whole damn thing on the teak coffee table.

Too bad his past couldn't be tucked away as easily.

He wrestled with where to start and figured what the hell. Might as well go back to the be-ginning.

Elbows on his knees, he rolled the water bottle between his palms. "You know what I did as a teenager, but I don't think I've ever really ex-plained why."

She sat up straighter, her forehead furrowing, but she didn't speak.

"A teenage boy is probably the dumbest cre-ation on the planet. Pair that with a big ego and no moral compass, and you've got a recipe for trouble."

Seventeen years later and he still couldn't get past the guilt of what he'd done.

"You were so young," she said softly.

"That's no excuse. I was out of control and hating life. This girl I liked had dumped me because her parents didn't want her around my family." He glanced at her. "Her dad was a cop. My ego stung. And I decided to show him and the justice system what screwups they were, because I—a teenager—was going to do what they couldn't. I would make the corrupt pay." Starting with two leches he'd caught hitting on his sister, damn near assaulting her, and his dad hadn't done more than shrug off his friends' behavior by insisting no harm, no foul.

"You had good intentions. All of the news reports I read said as much. And yes, I searched every one of them since you're usually close-mouthed about your past." She set aside her drink and clutched his forearm, squeezing. "While it's admirable you feel bad, you can also cut yourself some slack. You were exposing corrupt corporations."

"Not so much. See, I could have infiltrated my dad's records and those of his crooked friends, then turned them over to the authorities. And I could have had a better motivation than getting back at some girl or showing up my old man. But I wanted to make a statement. I wanted to make him see that even if I didn't do things his way, damn it, I was still every bit as smart. Because I would get away with it."

She didn't rush to reassure him this time, but she hadn't pulled away in disgust. Yet.

"Twisted, isn't it?" He set aside his water bottle to keep from shattering it in his fist. "I wanted to bring him—as well as a couple of his friends—down *and* make him proud of me."

"That had to make getting caught all the worse." She gathered a pillow to her, her voice steadier than her hands.

"That's the real kick in the ass irony." His hand fell to the lacy edge on the short sleeve of her nightgown and he rubbed it between two fingers. "I didn't get caught. I would have gotten away with it."

"Then how did you end up in reform school?"

"I found out that one of the CEOs of a business I'd helped tank with my short sales… He took his life." Acid fired at the lining of his stomach, burning up to his throat with a guilt that would never leave, no matter how many missions he completed or how much money he donated to charity. "I turned myself in to the police, with all the information on what I had done, everything I could dig up on my father."

"And the police gave you a more lenient sentence because you came forward." Her hand settled on his back, soothing. "What happened was horrible, but you did come forward with all that evidence, even when it incriminated you. That counts for something."

Laughter rumbled around in his chest, stirring the acid and mixing in some shards of glass for good measure to flay his insides. "Turning myself in didn't count for jack. I only got sent to that school instead of juvie because my dad hired the best lawyers. He got off of every major charge, and I could not beg my way into prison."

His dad's lawyers had made sure the press learned—through an "anonymous" leak—that every targeted company had been guilty of using child laborers in sweatshops overseas.

Once the media got wind of that part of his case, he'd been lauded the white knight of orphans. The pressure had nudged the judge the rest of the way in cutting him a deal. Through the colonel's mentorship, he and his friends had learned to channel their codes of right and wrong. Now they had the chance to right wrongs within the parameters of the law.

"I'm just damn lucky I landed in Salvatore's program. I owe him more than my life, Jayne." His voice strangled off with the emotion clogging his throat and squeezing his chest. "I owe him my self-respect."

Wordlessly she slipped her arms around him and pulled him to her. He pressed his forehead into her shoulder and drew in the pure, clean scent of her. She was too good for him, always had been. There just hadn't been anyone in her life to warn her away from him the way his teenage girlfriend's dad had.

"Conrad, Colonel Salvatore couldn't have built something within you if the foundation and all the essential parts weren't already there. You're a good man."

He didn't know how long they sat there, and a part of him knew he should let her go back to bed before he took anything more from her. But having her this close again felt better than he'd remembered, different, too. The glide of her fingers along the back of his neck soothed as much as they aroused. She was such a mix of contradictions, everything he wanted and all he didn't deserve.

She turned her face to graze a kiss across his temple before taking his face between her hands and looking him in the eyes. "I think we've both been hurting long enough."

Oh, God, this was it. The moment she would send him packing for good. She wouldn't wait around for him to sign the papers. She would pursue the divorce without his consent, an option that had always been open to her due to their lengthy separation. He hadn't realized until now how much hope he'd been holding on to. Like a sap, with every day that passed and no divorce, he'd allowed himself to believe there was a chance they would reconcile.

Now he had to face up to the fact that it was over between them, and she would move on to live the life she deserved. The one he'd never come close to offering her. She would find the man she deserved who would give her a real home and cute babies.

Forcing out words to set her free damn near split him in half. "Jayne, I never wanted to hurt you." He clasped her wrists, holding on to her for what would be the last time. "I only want you to be happy."

She angled back to stare deep in his eyes. "Then make love to me."

Eight

Leaning forward, her hip digging into the sofa cushions, Jayne skimmed her mouth over Conrad's, praying he wouldn't push her away again.

Desperate to see this through.

His admissions, his outpouring from deep in his soul only confirmed her conviction that he was a much better man than he realized. And regardless of whatever else had happened between them, she wasn't turning back from right now, right here with Conrad.

She sensed his restraint, his lingering concerns about protecting her from her dream or from herself. Whatever. To hell with holding back. She poured all her frustration and bottled emotions into the way her body ignited around him. Arching upward, she swung her leg around and over until she straddled him, bringing her flush against the hard length of his erection. She rocked once, twice, her hips to his until she felt the growl rumble in his chest. His arms shot up and around her, locking her to him.

A purr of relief spiraled up her throat.

"Jayne, are you sure this is what you want?" he asked between possessive kisses.

"Absolutely. We've both waited long enough. Stop talking and take me, damn it."

And thank heaven he listened and agreed. Angling her back onto the sofa, his solid body pressed her into the welcoming pile of pillows. He hooked a finger along the lacy edge of one sleeve, sliding along her shoulder and around until he skimmed her breast, launching delicious shivers of anticipation.

Desire surged liquid heat through her veins in a near-painful, all-over rush. She'd laid awake so many nights, aching for him, tempted to reach for the phone and just hear the sound of his voice. The rumbling timbre of him speaking her name then and now sent her spine bowing up toward him, as she wriggled to get closer.

She thumbed the buttons on his shirt free and yanked the fabric off his shoulders, sending it sailing to rest on a water bottle. Sighing, she splayed her fingers over his chest, up along his shoulders to pull him to her again. The heat of his bare flesh seared through her nightgown, her breasts tingling with awareness. How had she made it through the past three years without him, without this?

Her hand slid between them, down the front of his jeans, stroking his erection straining against his fly until he throbbed impossibly harder against her touch. She fumbled with the top button then eased the zipper down. Her fingers tucked inside his boxers, and he groaned low in his throat.

The steely length of him fit to her hand, familiar even after years apart. Although in some ways it seemed like no time at all, given all the hungry dreams she'd had of him coming to her bed again. Or in some of her more uninhibited fantasies he'd come to her in other places. Whisking her away from work to make love in the car. Joining her on a beach walk where they slipped behind a sand dune together. Or appearing next to her in a dark theater…

But she always woke up alone, unfulfilled and knowing he would never come for her. She had to move on with her life.

God, her thoughts were running away from her, threatening to steal this moment from them again.

Conrad shifted on top of her, and she gripped his shoulders to hold him in place. "Where are you going?"

"Jayne, I'm not leaving." His hands never stopped moving and arousing her even while he talked. "I packed a box of condoms in my suitcase, because even though I didn't just assume we would sleep together, I sure as hell wasn't going to lose the chance due to poor planning."

"Guess what?" She slid her hands around, digging her nails into his buttocks. "I'm a good planner, too."

"Then lucky for us, we have plenty to get through the night." He slid off her and stood, wearing nothing but his jeans, open and low slung on his hips in a tempting V. "So do I go get mine and come back, or do we move to the bedroom?"

Her brain was so fogged just staring at him that she struggled to form an answer. She didn't want to think. She just wanted to feel him over her, moving into her. But if they stayed here, there would be the awkward moment afterward when they pulled themselves together afterward and walked to separate bedrooms—which was insane, since she was his wife. For now at least.

And she realized exactly what she wanted. To be in his bed, to make love there and sleep in his arms.

"Let's go to your room."

Before she could say another word, he swept her against his chest in such a macho show of strength she smiled just before she flicked his earlobe with her tongue then drew it between her teeth, enjoying the slightly salty taste of him.

The lingering scent of his aftershave mixed with the musk of perspiration on his skin. She drew in the smell of him, the feel of him, until even the silk of her nightgown felt itchy against her oversensitized skin. The hard wall of his muscled chest wasn't the one of a paper pusher or a man who'd become soft from years of high living. He could take charge in every realm, intellectually and physically, and that duality turned her on all the more.

He shouldered open his door, revealing a massive teak bed sprawling in front of a window overlooking the river. Then she didn't see anything other than the linen drapes on the ceiling over the bed as he settled her in the middle of a simple cotton comforter. He angled to his suitcase on the stand, pulled out a box of condoms and tossed it on the bed before leaning over her again.

With competent and quick hands he bunched her gown in his fists and swept it away. The breeze over her skin made her want the press of his body but he sprinkled kisses along her stomach, took the edge of her bikini panties between his teeth and tugged. She thought of the panties he'd torn from her body in the elevator, of how he'd given her such an intense release.

At the first nuzzle between her legs, her knees fell apart and her bones turned to liquid. The flick of his tongue and gentle suckling brought her to the edge too fast, too soon. She clawed at his shoulders, drawing him up, but he stopped, teasing the tight nipple the way he'd licked and laved the tight bud of nerves.

He had her writhing on the comforter, aching to take this further, faster. His hand slid down to replace his tongue with a knowing touch. He inched his way back up her body until his mouth settled on her breast and his fingers between her legs teased in synchronicity, playing her perfectly. He knew her, just like the night at *La Bohème*. Except now she was naked and they were alone so he had free rein for more. He stroked the tight bundle of nerves with his thumb while sliding two fingers deep, crooking at just the right spot.

She gasped and pressed harder against his hand even as she wanted all of him. "No more playing. I just want you inside me."

"And you can be damn sure that's exactly where I want to be." He rolled her nipple lightly between his teeth. "But I want that—want you— so much and it's been so long, I'm not going to last. I need to take care of you first."

She circled him, stroking…her thumb rolling over the damp tip. And yes, she was every bit as close to coming apart.

"That works both ways you know, the part about having gone without sex for too damn long." She reached for the condom box and tugged free a packet. "No more waiting. If we come fast, then we get to linger later, but I can't wait anymore."

Determined to delay not a second longer, she sheathed him with a familiarity and newness that she still didn't quite comprehend. The fan rustled the curtains around their haven.

He held her face, looked into her eyes and said, "There hasn't been anyone since you. No one comes close to turning me inside out the way you do. And even when I resent it like hell, there's no denying it. I only want you."

His words stilled her hands. *No one* since her? For three years?

She wanted to believe him, ached to believe him. Because she felt the same. She even understood the part about resenting the way this feeling for each other took over her body and her life.

And then he kissed her. He thrust his tongue as he pushed inside her. Filling her, stretching her with more of that newness after so damn long away from each other. The sweet abrasion of his chest rasped along her nipples. The hard roped muscles of his legs flexed with each pump of his body. She dug her heels into the mattress and angled up against him until the gathering tension in her pulled even tighter, bringing her closer.

Her hand flung out to grab the headboard, the

intense sweetness was almost too much. She wanted to hang on to the sensations as tightly as she held the headboard, but he'd taken her too close to the edge with his mouth and his skillful touch.

One more deep stroke finished her. Pleasure rippled from her core, pulling through her, outward until the roots of her hair tingled. She bowed upward into him, even as her head thrashed on the pillow.

He chanted encouragement as her release pulsed and clamped around him, his voice growing hoarse until he hissed between gritted teeth. And while she'd doubted so much about their relationship, she knew he'd told her the truth about the past three years. He belonged to her.

She hugged him in the aftermath as he collapsed on top of her. The ceiling fan overhead click, click, clicked, gusts shifting the drapes around the towering teak bed. She trailed her fingers along his broad back, her foot up his thigh, and didn't take for granted the feel of him.

Not anymore.

It was one thing to be angry at him for the past thirty-six months. And another altogether to accept he'd been every bit as torn apart by their breakup as she had. With what he'd shared about his father tonight, she started to realize she'd never fully grasped what made him tick. Maybe if she dug for more clues about his relationship with his father in particular, she might understand how he'd arrived at his place of such emotional isolation.

Because she realized more than ever that she couldn't just walk away again.

Conrad held his wife spooned against him while she slept. She was back in his bed. He'd won.

And he didn't feel one bit peaceful about letting Jayne go.

Moonbeams reflected on the river water, the dock light glowing. If she was awake, he would have liked to sit out there with her and just listen to the night sounds, then walk with her up to the house, shower with her in the outdoor stall with the stars above them.

He'd made love to her twice more and still it wasn't enough. He rested his chin on her head, the sweat of their lovemaking lightly sealing their bodies, her spine against his chest. Each breath pressed her closer again, stirring his hard-on to a painful intensity. His hand slid around to cup her breast, filling his palm with her creamy roundness. She moaned in her sleep, her nipple drawing up into a tight bead.

She was in his blood. Rather than clearing away the past, making love with her had churned up all the frustration of the past three years. The thought of letting her go—unbearable. But he couldn't envision taking her back to Monte Carlo.

Although, how to blend her into his old life could be a moot point. If his cover had been blown, his Interpol work would be over. He angled to kiss her shoulder over the light red mark of his beard bristle from last night. He could have Jayne back and no more unexplained absences.

But the thought of ending his Interpol work... hell. He wouldn't have considered it before. Although since Zhutov might have taken that choice from him, he might as well make the best of the situation. And he couldn't just let Jayne wander off with God knows what kind of threat looming. These sorts of crooks did not forget.

His path became clear.

Protect Jayne.

His life came into focus. He realized his past mistake. He'd tried too hard to blend her into his world in Monte Carlo. He'd let her too close to the darker side of himself. Somehow, he must have known that, since he'd chosen to bring her here, to a place that represented the man he'd once wanted to be.

Jayne shifted in her sleep, arching her breast into his hand, her bottom wriggling against him. He throbbed against the sweet dip in her spine and the beginning of his need for her pearled along the tip of his erection. He clamped a hand on her stomach to hold her still.

Sighing, she looked back over her shoulder at him with sleepy half-awake eyes.

"Is it morning?" she asked in a groggy voice.

"Not yet. Keep sleeping." He had a packed day planned, showing her the full extent of the compound he'd built here. "We have plenty of time."

"Hmm... Except I'm not sleepy." She reached behind her to stroke his hair. "What's on the agenda for today?"

He nuzzled her hair. "I have some ideas. But what do you want?"

"At some point, breakfast. A very big breakfast, actually. After last night, I'll need more than pastries and tea."

"I'm certain I can figure something out."

"You cook?"

He was a little insulted by the assumption that he didn't, until he remembered all the times he'd burned toast when they were still together. His cooking was a more recently acquired skill. "I make some pretty fierce eggs Benedict these days."

"Sounds heavenly." Her head rested back against his chest. "I also noticed you've taken up redecorating."

Did he detect a note of pique in her voice? He opted for honesty. "Having your things around brought back too many memories. It was easier to move forward if I got rid of them."

Her feet tucked between his. "But you didn't replace everything. The red room stayed the same."

"That was the only room in the penthouse where we never had sex."

"So let me get this straight. You tossed out every piece of furniture that reminded you of the two of us having sex there."

"Pretty much."

She stayed silent, and he wished he could see her face to gauge her mood. So much of her was familiar and then other times not so much. She'd changed. So had he. They were both warier.

Finally she smiled back at him over her shoulder. "Good thing we never made love in the Bentley. It would have been a damn shame for you to have to get rid of such a cool collector's item."

"You have a point." He kissed her, wondering if he would have to burn this bed if she walked out on him again. "I guess we've both made some changes. What prompted you to swap from being an E.R. nurse to Hospice care?"

"You've obviously kept tabs on me. Why do you think?"

Was that a dig? "You know you don't have to work, right? No matter what happens between us, I will take care of you."

She flipped back the covers and started to sit up. "I don't need to be 'taken care of.'"

"Whoa… Hold on now." He looped an arm around her waist. "I didn't mean to offend you. I was just commenting on the fact that we're married. What's mine is yours. Fifty-fifty."

"Don't let your lawyer hear you give up your portfolio that easily."

"Not. Funny."

Still, she sat on the edge of the bed, the vulnerable curve of her back stirring his protective urges. She could shout her independence all day long. That wouldn't stop him from wanting to give her nice things. And more importantly, it wouldn't stop him from standing between her and anything that threatened her.

Shifting up onto an elbow, he rubbed her back and tried to backtrack, to fix what he'd screwed up. "Tell me about your new job."

Was it his imagination or did the defensive tensing of her shoulders ease?

"When I came back to Miami, my old job had obviously been filled. I took the Hospice opening as a temporary stopgap until a position more in my line of expertise became available. Except I found I didn't want to leave the job. It's not that I was unhappy with my work before, but something changed inside me."

"Like what?" He smoothed his hand down to the small of her back, the lolling of her head cluing him in to keep right on with the massage.

"I think I was drawn to E.R. work initially

because there wasn't as much of a chance of my heart being engaged." She glanced back. "I don't mean to say that I didn't care for the patients. But there wasn't time to form a relationship with someone who's out of your care in under an hour. I had a set amount of time to help that person, and then we moved on."

He massaged along the tendons in her neck. "Your dad's stunt hiding a second family really must have done a number on you."

"I had trouble connecting with others." She sagged back onto the bed and into his arms. "Now I find there's a deep satisfaction in bringing comfort to people when life is at its most difficult. It may sound strange…"

"Not at all," he said as he tucked her tight against him, this amazing woman he damn well didn't deserve but couldn't bring himself to give up.

"Enough depressing talk about the past. I don't know about you, but I can think of a far more enjoyable way to spend our time now that I am completely awake." She stretched out an arm to slide a condom from the bedside table and pressed it into his palm.

Smiling seductively over her shoulder, she skimmed her foot along his calf, her legs parting ever so slightly for him, inviting him. And call him a selfish bastard, but he wasn't one to turn down an invitation from Jayne. He'd been without her for so long he couldn't get enough of her. Time and time again he'd been tempted to fly to Miami and demand she come home.

Like that would have gone over well.

Instead he'd sent back those damn divorce papers repeatedly, knowing eventually she would have to come to him. She'd been well worth the wait. He skimmed his fingers around her again, slipped them down between the damp cleft, stroking as she opened farther.

With two fingers, he circled, faster, pressing and plucking with the amount of pressure he knew she enjoyed, bringing a fresh sigh from her. And just when he'd brought her to the edge, he hooked his arm under her knee and angled his sheathed erection just right, so close to everything he'd dreamed of and fantasized about when he'd taken those long and unsatisfying showers without her.

As he slid inside Jayne, *his wife,* he vowed he would not lose her. And he would never, never let anything from his past touch her again.

Jayne stood at the river's edge and watched the gazelle glide through the tall grasses on the other side of the mangrove swamp. The midmorning sun climbed up the horizon in a shimmering orange haze, echoing the warm glow inside her after a night of making love with Conrad.

Again and again. He'd given her explosive orgasms and foreplay to die for. He'd brought her a late-night snack in bed of flatbreads and meats, fed to each other. He'd fed her perfectly prepared eggs Benedict this morning. They'd talked and laughed, everything she'd dreamed could happen for them again.

How different might things have been if they'd come here for their first anniversary? If they'd

talked through all the things they were only beginning to touch on now?

And she couldn't completely blame him anymore. As she looked back, she accepted the
times she'd let things slide rather than push him,
because deep in her heart she was scared she
wouldn't be able to walk away.

Her mother hadn't deserved what happened to
her. God knows Jayne hadn't deserved it, either.

But she refused to be passive any longer. If—
and that was a *big* if—she and Conrad stood a
chance at patching things up, he needed to be
completely open with her. They needed a true
partnership of equals.

Glancing over her shoulder up to his home on
the plateau, she saw her husband pacing, talking on his cell phone. He'd said he needed to
check in with Salvatore before he took her on
a tour of the property. Apparently there were
other buildings and even a small town beyond
the rolling hills and she had to admit to curios-
ity about what drew him here. The home—the

whole locale—was so different from the glitz of his other holdings.

It gave her hope.

So much hope that she'd called Anthony. She'd arranged for a friend from work to pick up Mimi. If she was going to even consider making things work with Conrad, she had to cut off any ties to Anthony, a man she'd considered dating.

Watching Conrad walk down the incline toward her now, she wasn't ready to pack her things and bring Mimi across the ocean yet, but for the first time in three years, she was open to the possibility. She just needed the sign from Conrad that he would compromise this go-round.

He closed the distance between them, stopping at the shoreline with tall grasses swaying around his calves. He draped an arm around her shoulder. "Salvatore's staff is still wading through backlogs of visitors, letters, emails, any contact with the outside world. A suspicious amount of money was moved from Zhutov's wife's account.

Salvatore hopes to have concrete answers by the end of the day."

The threat sounded so surreal, but then Conrad's whole hidden career still felt strange to her. "What about Troy and Hillary?"

"They're safely in the Bahamas at a casino and no signs of anyone tracking them, either. By all accounts, they're enjoying the vacation of a lifetime."

"So this could all be a scare for nothing?"

He kissed her forehead. "Not nothing. We're here, together."

For how long? Long enough to find a path back together? She wished they could stand here by the river watching the hippo bathe himself in mud.

She tucked closer to Conrad's side, the sun beaming down on them. "Did you get any sleep last night?"

"Three or four hours. I'm good."

"Yes, you are." Turning in his arms, she kissed him good-morning and wondered just how private this spot might be. She looked at the dock, then up the incline at the deck and the outdoor shower stall. Her mind swirled with possibilities....

With a final kiss to her forehead, he angled back. "Ready to go for the tour?"

"Absolutely." Walking alongside him to the Land Cruiser, she tucked away her fantasy for another time, intensely curious about this tour and the opportunity to dig deeper into what made her husband tick.

The wilds of Africa were definitely a world away from Monte Carlo. Instead of flashy royalty in diamonds and furs, a spotted cheetah parted the grasslands not far from a mama giraffe with her baby. They walked with a long-legged grace much more elegant than any princess.

She rolled down her window, letting the muggy air clear away the images of the glitzier lifestyle, immersing herself in the present. "We know each other well in some ways and in others not at all—no dig meant by that. I feel like it's my fault, too."

"None of this is your fault. I'm the one responsible for my own choices and actions, no excuses from the past." Wind tunneled in his white polo shirt, his faded jeans fitting to his muscled thighs.

It wasn't about the clothes with him. She couldn't help but think—not for the first time— how he had a powerful presence just by existing, whether he was in a tuxedo in Monte Carlo or dressed for the desert realms of Africa.

She studied the hard line of his jaw, peppered with stubble. "Why can't you let me feel sorry for what you went through as a teenager?"

"I don't want sympathy. I want you naked." He shot a seductive grin her way. "We can pull over and…"

"You're trying to distract me." And she was determined to talk. "You promised to answer my questions."

Only the wind answered, whispering through the window as they drove toward a small cluster of buildings in the distance, with cars and lines of people, adults and kids. Perhaps this was a school?

Regardless, her time to talk would be cut short soon.

"Conrad? You promised," she pressed as birds ducked and dove toward their windshield only to break away at the last instant.

He winced, looking back at the narrow rural road. "You're right. I promised."

"Where did you stay on school breaks? Or did you stay at the school, like juvenile hall or something?"

The smile left his eyes. "I went home for holidays with an ankle monitor."

Thoughts of him as a teenager walking around with that monitoring device chilled her. "That had to have been awkward after you tried to turn in your father."

"My dad told me I could make it all up to him by connecting him with the families of my new friends." He steered around a pack of dwarf goats in the road. "Why don't we talk about your dad instead, Jayne?"

He guided the car back on the road again, leading them closer to the long stucco building, surrounded by smaller outbuildings. The slight detour off the road jounced her in the seat, hard, almost as if he'd deliberately bounced her around.

She held up her hands in surrender. "Okay, message received."

Her husband wasn't as open to talking this morning, but she wouldn't give up. She would simply wait for a better opening while they spent their day at... Not a school at all.

He'd driven her to a medical clinic.

Nine

Conrad watched his wife, curious as to what she would think of the clinic he'd built. Because yes, he'd built it as a tribute to her and the light she'd brought to his world. Regardless of how their marriage had broken up in the end, his four years with her were the best in his life.

She asked him all those questions about his father and the arrest, looking for ways to exonerate him because she had such a generous and forgiving heart. But she didn't seem to grasp he'd done the crime. He was guilty of a serious wrong, no justification.

His life now had to be devoted to a very narrow path of making things right. The small hospital was a part of that thanks to a mission to the region nearly four years ago that had left a mark on him. He'd been aiding in an investigation tracing heroin traffic through a casino in South Africa, the trail leading him up the coast. He wasn't an agent so much as a facilitator to lend effective covers and information about people in his wealthy world. They'd taken down the kingpin in that case, but Conrad hadn't felt the rush of victory.

Not that time.

His nights had been haunted by visions of the *Agberos,* street children and teens also known as "area boys." They were loosely organized gangs forced into crime. And no matter how many kingpins Conrad took out, another would slide into place. There was no Salvatore to look after those boys, to change their lives with a do-over.

Conrad opened Jayne's car door, her reaction so damn important to him right now that his chest went tight with each drag of air. Lines of patients filed into the door, locals wearing anything from jeans and T-shirts to colorful local cloths wrapped in a timeless way. They were here for anything from vaccinations to prenatal care to HIV/AIDS treatment.

The most gut-wrenching of all? The ones here for both prenatal care and HIV treatment. There was a desperate need here and he couldn't help everyone, but one at a time, he was doing his damnedest.

He wasn't a Salvatore sort, but he could at least give these kids some relief in their lives. He could make sure they grew up healthy, and those that couldn't would have a fighting chance against the HIV devastating so many lives in Africa.

Jayne placed her hand in his and stepped out of the SUV. "Interesting choice for an outing."

"I thought since you're a nurse, you would like to see the facility."

"It's so much more than I would have expected in such a rural community."

"It feeds into the population of three villages,

and there are patients who drive in from even farther."

She shaded her eyes against the sun, turning for the full three-hundred-and-sixty-degree view of everything from the one-story building to storage buildings. The place even had a playground, currently packed with young kids playing a loosely organized game of soccer, kicking up a cloud of dust around them. A brindle dog bounded along with them, jumping and racing for the ball, reminding him of little Mimi.

Patients arrived in cars and on foot, some wearing westernized clothes and others in brightly colored native wear. A delivery truck and ambulance were parked off to the side. Not brand-spanking-new, but well maintained.

They'd accomplished a lot here in a few short years.

He pointed to the doctor pushing through the front double doors. Conrad had given the doc a call to be on the lookout for them. "And here's our guide. Dr. Rowan Boothe."

Another former Salvatore protégé.

Jayne halted Conrad with a hand on his arm. "Is it okay if we just wander around? I don't want to get in anyone's way or disrupt anyone's routine."

The doctor stopped at the end of the walkway, stethoscope around his neck, hands in the pockets of his lab coat.

"Ma'am, don't worry about the tour. He owns the place." Boothe said it in a way that didn't sound like a compliment.

Not a surprise.

He and Boothe hadn't been friends—far from it. From day one, the sanctimonious do-gooder had kept to himself. Getting a read off him had been tough. On the one hand, he'd picked fights and then on the other, Boothe damn near martyred himself working community service hours.

The doc didn't much like Conrad, and Conrad didn't blame him. Conrad had given Boothe hell over his do-gooder attitude. But Conrad couldn't deny the guy's skill and his dedication. Boothe was the perfect fit for this place, and probably even a better fit for Jayne.

Damn.

Where the hell had that come from?

Suddenly it mattered too much to him that Jayne approve of the clinic. He was starting to want her to see him as the good guy and that was dangerous ground.

Damn it all to hell. He needed distance, or before he knew it, she would start asking more questions, probing around in his past for an honorability that just wasn't there.

"Jayne, you're in good hands here. I'm going to tend to some business."

Jayne's head was spinning as fast as the test tubes in the centrifuge. Her slip-on loafers squeaked along the pristine tile floors as she turned to follow Dr. Boothe into the corridor, her tour almost complete.

One wing held a thirty-bed hospital and the other wing housed a clinic. Not overly large, but all top-of-the-line and designed for efficiency. The antibacterial scent saturated each breath she took, the familiarity of the environment wrapping her in comfort.

She'd expected Conrad to romance her today. That's what Conrad did, big gifts and trips. He remembered her preferences from cream-filled pastries to Italian opera.

But this? He'd always seemed to think her nursing was just a job and she'd followed his lead, figuring someone else needed the job she would have taken up. She'd had plenty of money as his wife… But God, after six months, she'd become restless and by the end of the first year, she'd missed her job so much her teeth ached.

Walking down the center hall of the clinic, she couldn't stop thinking maybe he had seen her need there at the end, that he'd been planning this for her. Had she given up on them too soon?

Dr. Rowan Boothe continued his running monologue about the facilities and their focus on childhood immunizations as well as HIV/AIDS treatment and education.

She was impressed and curious. "You and

Conrad seem to know each other well. How did you meet?"

The doctor looked more like a retired model than a physician. But from what she'd heard so far, his expertise was undeniable. "We went to high school together."

North Carolina Military Prep? Was he the kind who'd gone in hopes of joining the military or because of a near brush with the law? Asking felt...rude. And then there was the whole Salvatore issue...an off-limits question altogether. "Hmm, it's nice when alumni can network."

He quirked a thick blond eyebrow as they passed the pharmacy. "Yes, I was one of the 'in trouble' crowd who now use their powers for good instead of evil."

"You have a sense of humor about it."

"That surprises you?" he asked as he held open the door for her, a burst of sunshine sending sparks in front of her eyes.

"What you face here, the tragic cases, the poverty, the limited resources and crime..." She stepped onto the front walkway, shading her eyes. Where was Conrad? "How can you keep that upbeat attitude under such crushing odds?"

"People are living longer here because of this clinic. Those children playing over there would have been dead by now without it." He gestured to a dozen or so boys kicking a soccer ball on a playground beside the clinic. "You said you're a Hospice nurse now, an E.R. nurse before that. You of all people should understand."

He had a point.

"You're right, of course." Her eyes adjusted to the stark sunshine and out there in the middle of the pack of boys, her husband joined in, kicking the soccer ball.

Laughing?

When was the last time she'd heard him laugh with something other than sarcasm? She couldn't remember. The sound of him, the *sight* of him, so relaxed took her breath away. He looked... young. Or rather he looked his age, a man in his early thirties, in the prime of life. Not that he'd looked old before but he'd been so distant and unapproachable.

She glanced at Dr. Boothe. "What was he like back in high school?"

"Moody. Arrogant. He was gangly and wore glasses back then, but he was a brilliant guy and he knew it. Folks called him Mr. Wall Street, because of his dad and what he did with the stock market." He glanced at her. "But you probably could have guessed all of that."

She just smiled, hoping he would keep talking if she didn't interrupt.

"I didn't come from money like most of the guys there, and I wasn't inordinately talented like Douglas. I had a monster chip on my shoulder. I thought I was better than those overprivileged brats. I caught a lucky break when I was sent there. I didn't fit in so I kept my distance." He half smiled. "The sense of humor's a skill I acquired later."

"Yet, Conrad brought you here. He must respect you."

"Yeah, I guess. I have the grades, but so do a lot of doctors who want to save the world. If we're going to be honest, I'm here because of a cookie."

"Pardon me? I'm not sure I understand."

"My mom used to send me these care packages full of peanut butter cookies with M&M's baked into them. Damn, they were good." The fond light in his eyes said more about the mother who sent the baked goods. "One day, I was in my bunk, knocking back a couple of those cookies while doing my macro-biology homework. And I looked up to find Conrad staring at those cookies like they were caviar. I knew better than to offer him one. He'd have just thrown it back in my face."

He leaned against a porch pillar. "We were all pretty angry at life in those days. But I had my cookies and letters from Mom to get me through the days when I didn't think I could live with the guilt of what I'd done."

He shook his head. "But back to Conrad. About a week later, I was on my way to the cafeteria when I saw him in the visitation area with his dad. I was jealous as hell since my folks couldn't afford to fly out to visit me—and then I realized he and his dad were fighting."

"About what?" She couldn't help but ask, desperate for this unfiltered look into the teenager Conrad had been during a time in his life that had so tremendously shaped the man he'd become.

"From what Conrad shouted, it was clear his father wanted him to run a scam on Troy's parents and convince them to invest in some bogus company or another. Conrad decked his dad. It took two security guards to pull him off."

The image of that betrayal, of the pain and humiliation he must have felt, brought tears to her eyes she knew her overly stoic husband would never have shed for himself. "And the cookie?"

"I'm getting there. Conrad spent a couple of days in the infirmary—his dad hit him back and dislocated Conrad's shoulder. The cops didn't press charges on the old man because the son threw the first punch. Anyhow, Conrad's first day out of the infirmary, I felt bad for him so I wrapped a cookie in a napkin and put it on his bunk. He didn't say anything, but he didn't toss it back in my face, either." He threw his hands wide. "And here I am today."

Her heart hurt so badly she could barely push words out. "You're killing me, you know that don't you?"

"Hey, don't get me wrong. He's still an arrogant ass, but he's a good guy if you dig deep." He grinned. "Really deep."

She looked back out at her husband playing ball with the kids. His voice rode the breeze as he shouted encouragement and tips, and she couldn't help but think of the father that had never been there for him. No wonder he was wary of being a parent himself.

But if he could only see himself now. He was such a natural.

She'd dreamed of them having children one day, and she'd hoped he could be a good father. But she'd never dared imagine him like this. She should be happy, hopeful.

Instead she was scared to death. It was one thing to fail at her second chance with Conrad if she would have had to walk away from the same failed marriage she'd left before. But everything was different this time. What if she lost the chance to make Conrad genuinely happy? This chance to touch lives together in Africa?

That would level her.

An older boy booted the soccer ball across the field, a couple of smaller boys chasing it down. The ball rolled farther away, toward a moving truck stacked with water jugs. The vehicle barreled along the dirt road without the least sign of slowing even as the child sprinted closer on skinny little legs.

Her heart leaped into her throat. Dr. Boothe sprang into motion but there was no way he would make it to the child in time.

"Conrad!" Jayne screamed, again and again.

But he was already sprinting toward the kid, who was maybe six or seven years old. Conrad moved like a sleek panther across the ball field, faster than should have been possible. And in a flash, he'd scooped the child up with one arm and stopped a full ten yards away from the truck. He spun the kid around, sunshine streaming down from the sky around them. The little boy's giggles carried on the breeze as if all was right in the world. And it was. Conrad had the situation firmly in hand.

Her heart hammered in her ears.

A low laugh pulled her attention away from her husband and back to Dr. Boothe. A blush burned up her face over being caught staring at her husband like a lovesick teenager.

God, her feelings for Conrad were so transparent a total stranger could read her.

What did her husband think when he looked at her? Did he think he'd won her over today? If so, she needed to be damn clear on that point. Yes, she was hopeful, but that didn't mean she was willing to compromise on her dreams.

But what about his dreams?

This close brush with danger revealed her husband's competence in a snapshot. She'd spent so many nights worried about why he hadn't called home, but seeing him in action gave her a new appreciation for how well equipped he was for quick action in risky work. He was smart, strong and he had resources. Furthermore, he had lightning reflexes and a will to help others.

Was she being as selfish as she'd once accused him of being by denying him a job that obviously meant a lot to him? A job that was, she now understood, a conduit to forgiving himself for his past? Clearly Conrad needed his work as badly as she needed hers.

That realization hurt, making her feel small and petty for all the accusations she'd hurled at him. He'd deserved better from her then, more understanding. She couldn't change the past and she didn't know if they had a future together or not.

But she could control what she did today.

Conrad started the Land Cruiser, sweat sticking his shirt to his back from the impromptu ball game and the surprise sprint to keep the little Kofi from dashing in front of a moving truck. His head still buzzed with the kick of fear when he'd seen the kid sprint toward the vehicle, unaware of anything but reaching that soccer ball.

Thank God the worst hadn't happened.

Playing with the kids was the high point of these visits for him, something he always did when he had time here. But today, he'd also needed the outlet after watching Jayne with Boothe, their heads tucked together as they discussed the ins and outs of the clinic.

The day had been a success in every way that mattered, and he was a petty bastard for his foul mood. He wanted to blame the stress on Zhutov, and God knows that added to his tension. There wasn't a damn thing he could do but wait until the enemy made a move. And once that wait was over?

Hell. The need to take his wife home and imprint himself in her memory, deep in her body, took hold of him. And he couldn't think of a reason why he shouldn't follow through on the urge to make love to her until they both fell into an exhausted sleep.

He put the car in Drive and accelerated out

of the parking lot. His wife sat beside him with that expression on her face again, like she'd put him under a microscope. He prepped for what he knew would come next.

"That was amazing how fast you reacted when the child ran toward that truck."

"I just did what anyone would have." And he'd also had a word with the truck driver about the dangers of speeding past a playground. "Kofi— the kid—spends a lot of time here with his older brother, Ade. Their mother comes regularly for her HIV treatments."

"Do you know all the kids' names?"

"Some," he answered noncommittally.

She sighed in exasperation. "You said before we got on the plane you would tell me anything. Did you mean that?"

"I should have put a limit on how many questions you could ask." A flock of geese scattered in front of him.

"I'll go easy on you then. What's your favorite kind of cookie? I realize I should already know that, and I feel awful for having to ask when you have my favorite pastry memorized, but I real-ized I really don't know."

Cookie? What the hell? "Um, anything with M&M's. I'm, uh, partial to M&M's in my cook-ies."

She smiled and touched his knee. Apparently he'd answered that one correctly.

"Next question?"

"Why don't you wear glasses anymore? And why didn't you ever mention that you used to? You'd think there would be pictures."

"Boothe," he said simply. Now he understood why they'd been standing under the awning so long. Boothe had been spouting out crap about the past. "I had Lasik surgery on my eyes so I don't need glasses anymore. As for photos of me wearing them? They perished in a horrible acci-dent, a trash can fire in Salvatore's office. A fire extinguisher was sacrificed in the line of duty."

Her hand stayed on his knee. "You have a sense of humor when you want to—sarcastic, sure but funny."

She stroked higher up his thigh and he damn

near drove into a ditch. He clasped her wrist and moved her back to her side of the car.

"You'll need to put that thought on hold."

Laughing softly, she hooked an elbow out the window, her blond hair streaking across her face. "I want to know more about your job with Interpol."

Apparently the easy questions had just been to soften him up.

"What do you want to know?"

"I keep trying to wrap my brain around the whole notion of you and your friends living a James Bond life, and it's blowing my mind. How did I miss guessing for four years?"

Because he was a damn good liar?

That didn't seem like a wise answer. He measured out a smarter answer, balancing it with what was safe to tell her.

"We're more freelancers, and we don't take jobs often. It actually keeps the risk of exposure down." But the longer he went between assignments, the more restless he grew. If this Zhutov case blew up in his face, would Salvatore cut him out or relegate him to some paper-pushing research? "I only worked six 'projects' in the entire time we were together. An assignment could take anywhere from a week to a month."

She nodded, going silent while she stared out the window at an ostrich running on pace with them at forty-two miles per hour. Her deep breath gave him only a flash of a notice that she wasn't giving up.

"Sounds to me like your Alpha Brotherhood has morphed into a Bond Brotherhood." She tipped her face into the wind, her eyes closed, her neck arched and vulnerable. "Troy is definitely the Pierce Brosnan Bond type, with his charm and his metro-sexual style. Malcolm is the Roger Moore type, old school Bond with his jazz flair. I only recall meeting Elliot Starc once, but he fits well enough for the Timothy Dalton slot, rarely seen but very international. The doctor, Boothe, he's the Daniel Craig Bond, the tortured soul."

"Who said Boothe was part of the Alpha Brotherhood?" And yes, he noticed she'd aptly insinuated they were all working for Salvatore as well, something he didn't intend to confirm.

"Just a guess." She glanced at him, her perceptive blue eyes making it clear she hadn't missed the nuance. "By the way, *you* are absolutely the Sean Connery Bond."

"I think you're paying me a compliment." He glanced over and found her staring at him with a familiar sensual glint.

He went hard at just a look from her—and the promise in her eyes.

"You're sexy, brooding, arrogant and too damn mesmerizing for your own good. It's not fair, you know."

"I'm not sure where you're going with this."

"Just that I can't resist you. Even now, I'm sitting here fighting the urge to jump you right here in the middle of nowhere. I'm trying to play it cool and logical because I don't want either of us to get hurt again."

"Can we go back to the Sean Connery discussion?" He hooked an arm around her and tugged her to his side.

She adjusted her seat belt and leaned against him. "I wonder sometimes if we were drawn to each other because of feeling like orphans."

He forced himself not to tense as she neatly shifted the conversation again. "We had parents."

"Don't be so literal."

"Don't be such a girl."

"Um, hello? I have breasts."

"Believe me." His hand slid along the generous curve. "I noticed."

"You're not paying attention." She linked fingers with him, stopping his caress.

He squeezed her hand, driving with the other hand down the deserted private road leading back to his house. "You have my complete and undivided attention."

"Good, because there will be a quiz afterward," she said smartly.

He nuzzled her hair, and wondered when just sitting beside her, holding her hand had become such an incredible turn on. "I've missed you."

"I've missed you, too." Her head fell to rest

on his shoulder. "That's what I was getting at. You have your brotherhood, but you lead these separate lives with just periodic high octane reunions. Day by day, neither of us has a family."

He laughed darkly. "Dysfunctional is drawn to dysfunctional, I guess."

"Not exactly how I would have phrased it, but that works well enough." Her hand fell to rest on his knee, stroking lightly.

To arouse or soothe?

"Jayne, your dad's a loser just like mine was." Anger simmered in his gut over how her father had hurt her. "End of story. We overcame it."

"Did we?" She drew circles on his jeans, her touch heating him through the denim. "Or are we still letting them control our lives?"

His hand clenched around the steering wheel. He wanted to be with her, but damn it, she needed to leave discussions of his father in the past. He'd said all he cared to say about the old man who didn't warrant his time. This whole twenty questions game was officially over.

"If I wanted therapy I would pay a shrink." He

turned off the road, hitting the remote for the gate, which also triggered a timed release for the other layers of security along with a facial recognition program.

"Wow, Conrad," she said, sliding back to her side of the vehicle, "that was rude."

He reined his temper in even as sweat beaded his brow. "You're right." He stopped the car beside the house. "Of course."

"If you don't agree," she snapped, throwing her door open wide, "then just say so."

"I disagree, and I'm rude." He threw his arms wide as he circled to the front of the car. "I agree, and you tell me not to?"

"I just meant disagree politely." She crossed her arms over her chest, plumping her breasts in the simple white T-shirt.

His hard-on throbbed in his jeans, aching as much as the pain behind his eyes.

"I just want to get a shower and some lunch." He yanked his sticky polo shirt off and pitched it on the porch. To hell with this. He stalked toward the outside shower stall along the side of the house. "Not pick a fight."

"Who's picking a fight?" Her voice rose and she all but stomped a foot. "Not me. I'm just trying to have an honest discussion with you."

"Honest?" He barely kept his voice under control. That shower was sounding better and better by the second. Maybe it would cool down his temper. "You want to talk honest then let's talk about why you want to rewrite history so I'm some pathetic sap who blames the world for all his problems."

She stalked closer to him one step at a time until she stopped an inch shy of her breasts skimming his bare chest. "Conrad? Shut up and take me to the shower."

Ten

As much as Jayne ached to find answers that would give them a path to reconciliation, clearly Conrad didn't want to talk anymore. And to be honest with herself, the trip to the clinic had left her more than a little vulnerable. She'd seen a side to her husband she hadn't known existed. Beyond just funding a building, he was obviously hands-on at the place, well-known and liked. The way he'd played with the kids still tugged at her heart until she could barely breathe.

She definitely needed to give them both time and space. She was a patient woman, and right now she could think of the perfect way to pass that time.

Making love to her husband.

And if she was using sex to delay the inevitable? Then so be it. She couldn't leave the protection of this place so she might as well make the most of this time.

She linked fingers with Conrad and tugged him toward the side of the house.

"Jayne, the front door's that way."

"And the exterior shower is this way." She walked backward, pulling him with her. "Unless there's some reason we should stay inside? I figured since we walked around the grounds earlier, the security system outside is as good as inside."

"You are correct. I wouldn't have built an outdoor shower if it wasn't safe to use it. No one can get within a mile of this place without my knowing about it." He reassured her with a fierce protectiveness in his voice and eyes.

The magnitude of that comforted her and unsettled her at the same time. She was a dentist's kid from Miami. Prior to meeting Conrad, the extent of her security knowledge included memorizing the pin code for the security box on the garage leading into her condo.

She shoved aside distracting thoughts and focused on the now. Seducing Conrad. She pulled a condom from her purse and tucked it into his hand. "And that takes care of our last concern."

He flipped the packet between his fingers. "You were planning this all day?"

"Actually—" she tossed aside her purse "—I intended to get you to pull over on a deserted side road—since this whole place is essentially deserted that wouldn't have been tough—and I would seduce you in the car. Since the Land Cruiser is conveniently roomy, we would finish off the fantasy we started in the Jaguar in Monte Carlo."

He jerked a thumb over his shoulder. "Do you want to go back to the car?"

"I want you. In the shower. Now."

He hooked his thumbs in her jeans. "Happy to accommodate."

She grabbed the hem of her T-shirt and peeled it over her head, baring her white lacy bra. Late afternoon rays heated her skin almost as much as his eyes as she toed off her canvas loafers. The gritty earth was warm beneath her feet, pebbles digging into her toes.

Her hands fell to her belt buckle, and she unfastened her jeans, never taking her eyes from his sun-burnished face. She wriggled denim down her hips, enjoying the way his gaze stroked along each patch of revealed flesh. One last shimmy and she kicked aside her jeans, grateful she'd invested in new satin and lace lingerie before this trip.

That panty set forced her to admit she'd been hoping for just this when she'd come to Monte Carlo to deliver her five-carat ring and divorce papers. Deep in her heart, she'd hoped he would tear up the papers and slide the ring back on her hand.

Life was never that clear-cut. Today's answers had shown her more than ever how far more complex the situation—and her husband were.

But one thing was crystal clear. She had amazing lingerie and her husband's interest. And she intended to enjoy the hell out of their afternoon together.

She teased the front clasp open and tossed her bra aside. The extravagant scrap of satin and lace landed on top of her jeans. After they'd met in Miami, he'd rented a yacht to live on while he concocted business reasons to stay in town. Even though she'd been tempted to sleep with him from the first date, she'd held back, overwhelmed by his wealth, concerned about his past. But two months into the relationship, she couldn't ignore her heart any longer. She'd fallen irrevocably in love with him.

They'd made love on his yacht that night. They'd eloped four weeks later.

Memories of the optimism of that day and the heartbreak that followed threatened to chill her passion. She refused to let that happen, damn it.

Turning toward the shower, she called over her shoulder, "Someone's way overdressed for this party."

His eyes took on a predatory gleam, and he walked toward her, taking off his jeans and boxers with a speed and efficiency that sent a thrill of anticipation through her.

He stalked toward her, his erection straining hard and thick up his stomach. She reached behind her, her fingers grazing along the teak cubicle until she found the latch. She pulled the door open.

The slate tile floor cooled her feet after the scorched earth outside. She turned on the shower just as Conrad filled the entrance with his big, bold presence. The spray hit her in a cold blast, and she squealed, jumping back.

Laughing, Conrad stepped deeper inside, hooking an arm around her waist and hauling her against the delicious heat of his body until the spray warmed. She arched up on her toes to meet his kiss, water slicking over her skin in thousands of liquid caresses. She knew they couldn't continue like this forever. They were merely delaying the inevitable decision on where to take their relationship next.

That only made her all the more determined to indulge in every moment now. She scored her nails lightly down his back, down to his hips, her fingers digging into his flanks to urge him closer. The rigid press of his arousal against her stomach brought an ache and moisture between her thighs that had nothing to do with the sheeting water.

He caressed her back, her breasts, even her arms, the rasp of his callused fingertips turning every patch of her skin into an erogenous zone. One of his hands fell away, and she moaned against his mouth.

"Patience," he answered, his hand coming back into sight cupping a bottle of shampoo.

He raised his arm and poured a stream onto her head before setting aside the bottle. Suds bubbled, dripping, and she squeezed her eyes shut a second before he gathered her hair and worked up a lather. Pure bliss.

The firm pressure of his fingers along her scalp was bone melting. She slumped against the sleekly varnished walls. With her eyes closed, her world narrowed to the sound of the shower, the wind, the distant cackle of monkeys, a natural symphony as magnificent as any opera.

Certainly Conrad played her body well, with nuances from his massage along her temples to the outlining of her ears. Bubbles rolled down her body, slithering over her breasts and between her legs. She rubbed her foot along the back of his calf, opening her legs wider for the press of his erection against the tight bud of nerves already flaming to life. Each roll of her hips, each thrust of his fingers into her hair took her higher, faster.

The pleasures of the whole incredible day gathered, fueling the tingling inside her. He'd always been a generous lover and their chemistry had been explosive from their first time together. She opened her eyes and found him watching her every reaction.

Time for *her* to take *him*.

She scooped the bar of soap from the dish and worked up a lather. He lifted an eyebrow a second before she used her hands as the washcloth over his chest, down his sculpted arms and down to stroke his erection, cupping the weight of him in her hands. He twitched in her clasp, bracing a hand against the shower wall.

He clamped her hand to stop her.

"Jayne—" his voice came out choked and hoarse "—you're killing me."

"As I recall…" She sipped water from his chest, her tongue flicking around the flat circle of his nipple. "You never complained in the past when I took the initiative."

"True enough." He skimmed his hand over her hair, palming the back of her head.

"Then why won't you let me…"

He stepped back, the shower spraying between them. "Because you've called the shots for the past three years."

That was debatable, given how many times he'd sent her papers back unsigned. "Then this is a punishment? I'm not sure I like the context of that mixed with what's happening between us."

"Do you want to stop?" His question was simple enough, but the somber tone of his voice added weight and layers.

They were talking about the future. She wasn't ready to have this discussion with him.

"You know I don't want to stop. I never have. How about my turn now, yours later?" Clamping hands on his shoulders, she nudged him down to the shower seat. "Any objections to that?"

"None that come to mind." He spread his arms wide. "I'm all yours."

"Glad to hear it."

Anticipation curled through her. Kneeling in front of him, she took him in her mouth, the shower sheeting along her back. She gripped his thighs. The flex of muscles thrilled her as she took in every sign of his arousal increasing. His head thudded back against the cubicle wall, and yes, she delighted in tormenting him as much as he'd teased her last night, drawing out the pleasure.

She knew his body as well as he knew hers, thanks to years of great sex and exploring what drove the other crazy. And she drew on every bit of that stored knowledge now until his fist clenched in her hair, gently guiding her off him. She smiled, reveling in the powerful attraction, the connection that couldn't be denied even after three years apart.

His hands slid under her arms, and he lifted her onto his lap. She straddled him, the tip of him nudging between her legs, and she almost said to hell with birth control. Never had she been more tempted, her womb aching to be filled with his child. Aching to have a whole damn soccer team with this man. But after what her parents had put her through, she wouldn't risk bringing a child into an unstable relationship.

And, damn it, even thinking about those lost dreams threatened to wreck the mood. She grabbed the condom from the soap dish and passed it to him. Her hands were shaking too much to be of any help.

Her hands braced on his shoulders, and she raised up on her knees, taking him deep, deeper still inside her, lifting again. She slid her breasts up and down his chest. Every brush of flesh against flesh launched a fresh wash of goose bumps over her. Faster and faster they moved, his hands on her hips, guiding her as he thrust in synch with her.

Moans rolled up her throat, wrung from her, each breathy groan answered by him. And yes, she took added pleasure in controlling this much of her life, bringing him to the edge, knowing that his feelings for her were as all-consuming as her own were for him.

His hands slid under her bottom and he stood, never losing contact, their bodies still linked. He pressed her back to the wall, driving into her, sending her the rest of the way into a shattering orgasm. Her arms locked around him, her head on his shoulder as her cries of completion rippled through her.

Thank goodness he held her because she couldn't have stood. Even now, her legs melted down him, her toes touching the slate floor. His hot breath drifted through her hair as he held her in the aftermath of their release.

They'd made love in a shower numerous times

and the tub, too, but never in an outdoor shower. His adventurous nature had always appealed to her. She'd always been such a cautious, practical soul—her mother had always been so stressed, Jayne had worked overtime to be the perfect daughter and that regimen eventually became habit. Rigid attention to detail was a great trait for a nurse, but not in her personal life. Then Conrad had burst into her world.

Or rather he'd hobbled into the E.R. on that broken foot, stubbornly refusing to acknowledge just how badly he'd been hurt. Even in a cast, he'd been more active than any human she'd met. He'd swept her off her feet, and for the first time in longer than she could remember, she'd done something impulsive.

She'd married Conrad after only knowing him for three months.

If they'd dated longer might they have worked through more of these issues ahead of time? Had a stronger start to their marriage, a better foundation?

Or would she have talked herself out of marrying him?

The thought of having never been his wife cut through her. She wanted a future with him. She couldn't deny that, but she also couldn't ignore what a tenuous peace they'd found here.

And the least bump in the road could shatter everything.

Conrad lounged on the shower bench with the door open, watching his wife tug her clothes back onto her damp body. Damn shame they couldn't just stay naked, making love until the world righted itself again. "I read once that 'The finest clothing made is a person's skin, but, of course, society demands something more than this.'"

She tugged her T-shirt over her head, white cotton sticking to her wet skin and turning translucent in spotty places. "Where did you read that?"

"Believe it or not, Mark Twain."

"I always think of you as a numbers man."

She pulled her hair free of the neckline, stirring memories of washing her, feeling her, breathing in the scent of her.

Her legs glowed with a golden haze, backlit by the sunset. There was still time left in this day.

He gave her a lazy smile. "You've been thinking of me, have you?"

"I do. Often." Her smile was tinged with so much sadness it socked him right in the conscience.

He stood and left the shower stall, sealing the door after him. He reached for his jeans. "And where do you think of me? Somewhere like in bed? Or in the shower? Because I thought of you often in the shower and now..."

She rolled her eyes. "Where doesn't matter."

"It's been a long three years without you. I'm making up for lost time here." He tried to lighten the mood again, to bring them back around to level ground. "That's a lot of fantasies to work through."

"If only we could just have sex for the rest of our lives. That would probably cure your insomnia." She gave her jeans an extra tug up her damp legs, her breasts moving enticingly under the T-shirt.

She'd been his wife for seven years and still his mouth watered when he looked at her. Her blond hair was slicked back wet, her face free of makeup, and she was the most beautiful woman he'd ever seen.

"The last thing I think about when I'm with you is sleep." What a hell of a time to remember how their marriage had cured his insomnia in the beginning.

"Eventually we would wear out." She sauntered up to him and buttoned his jeans with slow deliberation, her knuckles grazing his stomach.

"Is that a challenge?" His abs contracted in response to the simple brush of her fingers against him.

And he could see she knew that.

She patted his chest before stepping back. "You enjoy a challenge. Admit it."

He grabbed her hips, hauled her against him and took her mouth. He would eat supper off her naked body tonight, he vowed to himself. He would win her over and bring her into his life again, come hell or high water. The past three years without her had been hell. The thought of even three days away from her was more than he could wrap his brain around.

The possibility that he might not be able to persuade her started a ringing in his ears that damn near deafened him. A ringing that persisted until he realized…

Jayne pulled back, her mouth kissed plump and damp. "That's my cell phone. I should at least check who it is."

Disappointment bit him in his conscience as well as his overrevved libido. "Of course you should."

She snatched her purse from the ground and fished out her cell phone. She checked the screen and frowned before pushing the button. "Yes, Anthony? What can I do for you?"

Anthony Collins? Conrad froze halfway down to pick up his polo shirt off the ground. What the hell was the man doing still calling Jayne? She said she'd ended any possible thoughts of romance between the two of them.

The way her eyes shifted away, looking anywhere but at Conrad wasn't reassuring, either. He didn't want to be a jealous bastard. He'd always considered himself more logical than that. But the thought of Jayne with some other guy was chewing him up inside.

She turned her back and walked away, her voice only a soft mumble.

Crap. He snatched his shirt off the ground and shook out the sand. He stood alone, barefoot, in the dirt and thought of all the times he'd isolated Jayne, cut her off from his world without a word of reassurance. He was a bastard. Plain and simple. She'd deserved better from him then and now.

Jayne turned around, and he willed back questions he'd given up the right to ask. He braced himself for whatever she had to say.

"Conrad." Her voice trembled. "Anthony said he's been getting calls from strangers claiming to be conducting a background check on me for a job I applied for. It could be nothing, but he said something about the questions set off alarms. He wondered if it might be someone trying to steal my identity. But you and I know, it could be so much worse than that…."

Her voice trailed off. She didn't need to state the obvious. His mind was already shutting down emotion and revving into high gear, churning through options for their next move.

And most of all how to make sure Jayne's safety hadn't been compromised.

Up to now his gut had told him Zhutov didn't have a thing on him. He didn't make mistakes on the job. But he couldn't ignore the possibility of Zhutov's reach when it came to Jayne so he'd been aggressively cautious.

Had he been cautious enough? Or had something slipped through the cracks while he was lusting after his wife? He shut down his emotions and started toward the house.

"We need to get inside now. I have to call Colonel Salvatore."

Jayne hated feeling useless, but what could she do? She wasn't some secret agent. Hell, she didn't even have her car or access to anything. She felt like she'd been turned into an ornamental houseplant—again.

Conrad had locked the house down tight before going to the panic room to talk to Salvatore and access his computers. She padded around the kitchen putting together something for supper while listening to one side of the phone conversation, which told her absolutely nothing.

Only a couple of hours ago, he'd shown her the clinic and it was clear he'd been trying to reach out to her by sharing that side of his life. Although the spontaneous soccer game had touched her just as much.

She tugged open the refrigerator and pulled out a container of Waldorf salad to go with the flaky croissants on the counter. And she vowed, if she found one more of her favorite anything already waiting here for her she would scream.

How could the man have ignored her for three years and still remember every detail about her food preferences? For three long years her heart had broken over him. She would have given any-

thing for a phone call, an email, or God, a surprise appearance on her doorstep. Did he really
think they could just pick up where they left off
now?

She spooned the salad onto plates, her hands
shaking and the chicken plopping on the china
with more than a little extra force. Would he
have continued this standoff indefinitely if she
hadn't come to him? She couldn't deny she loved
him and wanted to be with him, but she didn't
know if she could live the rest of her life being
shut out this way.

Slumping back against the counter, she squeezed
her eyes shut and forced herself to breathe evenly.
She thought about that teenage Conrad whose
trust had been so horribly abused by his father.
Conrad, who'd grown into a man who built a
health clinic and devoted his life to a job he could
never claim recognition for doing.

Boothe was right. Conrad was a good man.

She just needed to be patient. And instead of
peppering him with questions nonstop, she could
start offering him parts of her past, things that

were important but that she'd been hesitant to dredge up. But, good God, if she couldn't tell her husband, who could she talk to?

Yes, she still loved Conrad, but she wasn't the same woman she'd been three years ago. She was self-reliant with a clear vision for her future and a sense of her own self-worth.

She also knew that her husband needed her, whether he realized it or not. Pushing her own fears aside, she opened a bakery box full of cookies.

No matter how hard he worked to shut down emotions, still he couldn't ignore the weight of Jayne's eyes on him, counting on him. At least they had one less thing to worry about.

He leaned against the kitchen doorway. "Salvatore's looking into the calls, but so far he said everything looks on the up-and-up. He's confident it was just a hiring company for a hospital running a background check."

"Thank God. What a relief." Her eyes closed for an instant, before she scooped up two plates off the counter. "I made us something to eat. We missed lunch. Could you pour us something to drink?"

She walked past him, both plates of food in her hands. He opened a bottle of springwater, poured it into two glasses with ice then followed her into the dining room. Already, she sat at her place, fidgeting with her napkin.

No wonder she was on edge. All the pleasure of their day out, even making love in the shower, had been wrecked with a cold splash of reality. He sat across from her and shoveled in the food more out of habit than any appetite.

Jayne jabbed at the bits of apple in her salad. "Did I ever tell you why I'm such an opera buff?"

He glanced up from his food, wondering where in the world that question had come from. But then he had given up trying to understand this woman. "I don't believe you did."

"I always knew my parents didn't have a great marriage. That doesn't excuse what my father did to us—or to the family he kept on the side.

But my parents' divorce wasn't a huge surprise. They argued. A lot."

He set his fork aside, his full attention on her. "That had to have been tough for you to hear."

"It was. So I started turning on the radio to drown them out." She shrugged, pulling her hair back in her fist. "Opera worked the best. By the time they officially split, I knew all the lyrics to everything from *Madame Butterfly* to *Carmen*."

The image of her as a little girl sitting in the middle of her bed singing *Madame Butterfly* made him want to time travel to take her bike riding the hell away from there. But was he doing any better at protecting her in the present?

She leaned forward on her elbows. "Just so we're clear, you have absolutely no reason to be jealous of Anthony. Nothing happened with him, and I made sure he understood that when I spoke to him yesterday. I even had a friend from work pick up Mimi. I would never, never betray your trust that way."

"I believe you." And he did. He knew how she

felt about what her family had been through with her father's longtime affair.

"What's wrong then?" She clasped his arms, holding on tight, her eyes confused, hurt and even a little angry. "Why are you so…distant? You know those walls destroyed us last time."

He shoved away from the table, holding himself in check. Barely. But he wouldn't be like her father, shouting and scaring the hell out of her. "This whole mess with Zhutov and you having to second-guess every call that comes into your life. Do you expect me to be happy that there are people asking around about you? That I had to take you to a remote corner of the world to make sure no one is after you—because of me?"

"Of course you have a right to be worried, but if Colonel Salvatore says there's nothing to worry about, I believe him."

"Nothing to worry about—this time."

"We don't always have to assume the worst here."

A siren split the air like a knife, cutting her off midsentence.

He recognized the sound all too well. Someone had tripped the alarm on the outer edges of his property.

Holy crap. His body went into action, his first and only priority? Securing Jayne.

"Conrad?" Her face paled with panic. "What's that?"

"The security system has been tripped. Someone's trying to break into the compound." He grabbed her by the shoulders and hustled her toward the front steps. "You need to lock yourself in the panic room. Now."

Eleven

Jayne hugged her knees, sitting on a sofa in the panic room. Her teeth chattered with fear for her husband. She'd barely had time to process Anthony's confusing call before the alarm had blared. Conrad had hooked an arm around her waist, rushed her indoors and opened the panic room. He ushered her in and passed over a card with instructions for how to leave…

If he didn't return…

Horror squeezed her heart in an icy fist with each minute that ticked by. She'd already been in here for what felt like hours, but the clock on her cell phone indicated it had only been sixteen minutes.

Someone was trying to break in and there was nothing she could do except sit in this windowless prison while the man she loved faced heaven only knew what kind of danger. Desperately, she wanted to be out there with him, beside him. But Colonel Salvatore had been right. She was Conrad's Achilles' heel. If he had to worry about her, he would be distracted.

She understood that problem well.

There wasn't anything she could do now other than get her bearings and be on guard. Surveying the inside of her "cell," she took it in, for all the good that did her.

As far as prisons went it wasn't that bad, much like an efficiency apartment, minus windows and with only two doors—one leading out and the other open to a small bathroom. A bed filled a corner, a kitchenette with a table in another. A table and television rounded out the decor.

A television? She couldn't envision anyone in a panic room hanging out watching their DVD collection. Angling sideways, she grabbed the re-mote control off the end table. She turned on the TV. A view of the front yard filled the flat screen.

Oh, my God, she was holding the remote to a surveillance system. She wasn't isolated after all. Relief melted through her. She could help by monitoring the outside. She yanked her cell phone from her pocket and saw…she still had a signal so the safe room hadn't blocked her out.

She thumbed through the remote until she fig-ured out how to adjust the views—front yard, sides, the river—all empty. Her eyes glued to this thin connection to Conrad, she clicked again to a view of the outward perimeter including the clinic.

Not empty.

In fact, a small crowd gathered outside, even this late in the day with the sun setting fast. In the middle of the crowd, four lanky figures sat with their hands cuffed behind their backs.

Teenagers.

Probably not more than fifteen.

And if she guessed correctly, they were some

of the same kids who'd played soccer with Conrad just that afternoon.

She clicked the remote, the camera scanning the view until she found Conrad standing with Dr. Boothe. Her husband had his phone out, talking to the doctor while thumbing the keypad. She sagged back on the sofa. If there was any danger to her here, Conrad wouldn't be so far away.

Still, she stayed immobile, waiting for his call. She wouldn't be the fool in the horror films who walked right into a killer's path in spite of all the warnings. But how many times in her life had she sat waiting and worrying, unable to connect or help? She couldn't be a helpless damsel in distress or a passive bystander in her own life.

Her cell phone buzzed beside her, and she saw an incoming text from Conrad.

All clear. Just a break-in at the clinic for drugs. I'll be home soon.

A moment of sheer fright was over in an instant. Was this how Conrad lived on the job?

Not fun by any stretch of the meaning. But then, not any more stressful than the time she'd been working in the E.R. when a patient pulled a knife and demanded she empty the medicine cabinet. He'd been too coked up to hold the knife steady, and the security guard had disarmed him.

There weren't any guarantees in life, regardless of where she lived.

She picked up the clearance code and punched in the numbers to open the door back into the house. She texted Conrad an update.

Made it out of the panic room. No problems with the code.

She hesitated at the urge to type "love you" and instead opted for...

Be safe.

Seconds later the phone buzzed in her hand with an incoming text.

This will take a while. Don't wait up.

Not so much as a hint of affection coated that stark message, but then what did she expect? He was in the middle of a crisis. She shook off the creeping sense of premonition.

For a second, she considered returning to the panic room and just watching him on the screen, but that seemed like an invasion of his privacy. If she wanted this relationship to work between them, she needed to learn to trust him while he was gone. And he needed to learn to trust that she could handle the lifestyle.

So what did a woman do while her man was out saving the world? Maybe she didn't need all the answers yet. She just needed to know that she was committed to figuring them out.

She knew one fact for certain. Living without Conrad was out of the question.

The moon rose over the clinic, lights blazing in a day that had run far too long. Bile burned his throat as he watched the last of the *Agberos* loaded into a police car. Ade, a teen from the soccer game, stared over the door at him with defiant eyes that Conrad recognized well. He'd seen the same look staring back at him in the mirror as teenager.

Jayne and the house were safe, but four teens he'd played with just this afternoon had tried to steal drugs from the clinic. While one of them tried to escape, he'd strayed too close to the house. Boothe had said the attempts were commonplace. *Agberos* weren't rehabilitated in a day—and many of the Area Boys could never be trusted.

Now wasn't that a kick in the ass?

Intellectually he understood what Boothe had told him a million times. In a country riddled with poverty and lawlessness, saving even a handful of these boys was a major victory.

Still, defeat piled on his shoulders like sandbags.

The ringleader of this raid really got to him. Conrad had played soccer with Ade and his younger brother Kofi earlier. He thought he'd connected with them both. And yeah, he'd identified with Ade, seen the seething frustration inside the teen, and wanted to help him build a stable life for himself. Would the little Kofi follow in his big brother's footsteps?

There wasn't a damn thing more Conrad could do about it tonight. He jerked open the door to the Land Cruiser, hoping Jayne had turned in for the night, because he wasn't in the mood for any soul searching.

The drive home passed in a blur with none of his regular pleasure in the starkly majestic landscape that had drawn him to this country in the first place.

Ahead, his house glowed with lights.

The house where Jayne waited for him, obviously wide-awake if the bright windows were anything to judge by.

Conrad steered the Land Cruiser along the dirt road leading up the plateau, his teeth on edge and his temper rotten as hell. He floored the Land Cruiser, the shock absorbers working overtime. He couldn't put enough space between him and the mess at the clinic, now that the cops had everything locked down tight again.

He parked the Land Cruiser in front of the house, but left the car in idle. He couldn't just sit here thoughtlessly losing himself in his wife's softness in order to avoid the obvious. He needed to take action, to do something to resolve the questions surrounding Zhutov. And he needed to tuck Jayne somewhere safe—most likely somewhere far the hell away from anything in his world since his judgment was crap these days.

Bringing her here had been a selfish choice. He'd wanted to be alone with her. Like some kid showing off an A-plus art project, he'd wanted her to see his clinic, to prove to her there was something good inside him. There were plenty of other places she could stay that were safer. He would talk to Salvatore once Jayne was settled for the night.

He turned off the car, leaped out and slammed the door. Already, he could see her inside on the sofa, lamps shining. He should have tinted these windows rather than depending on the security system.

Just as he hit the bottom step, Jayne opened

the front door. Her smile cut right through him with a fresh swipe of guilt.

"Welcome back." She leaned in the open door, a mug of tea cradled in her hands. "What a crazy evening. But at least you know your security system works as advertised."

"You figured out how to work the surveillance television?" If so, that should cut down on the questions for tonight, a good thing given his raw-as-hell gut.

"I did, although I'm still a bit fuzzy on the details." She followed him inside, the weight of her gaze heavy on his shoulders.

"Some of the local *Agberos* tried to steal some drugs from the clinic. When the alarms went off at the clinic, one of the kids—Ade—ran away and tripped the security system here."

"Thank goodness they didn't get away with it. And I'm glad everything was resolved without anyone getting hurt."

"A guard was injured during the break-in." He pinched the bridge of his nose, pacing restlessly past a ladder against the wall covered with locally woven blankets. He needed to get to his computer, to plug into the network and start running leads.

"Oh, no, Conrad. I'm so sorry." Her hand fell to rest on his shoulder. "Will he be all right? Do they need my help at the clinic? I'm sorry now that I didn't go with you."

Her touch made him restless, vulnerable.

He walked to the window, looking out over the river. "You were here, safe. That's the best thing you could do for me."

"What's wrong?" She stopped beside him. "Why are you avoiding me?"

Because if he lost himself in her arms right now, he would shatter, damn it. His hands clenched. "This isn't the right time to talk."

She sighed, a tic tugging at the corner of her eye. "It's never the right time for my questions. That's a big part of what broke us up before." She squeezed his forearm. "I need for you to communicate with me."

Her cool fingers on his skin were a temptation, no question. She'd always been his weakness from the day he'd met her.

"I would rather wait for any discussion until we get the report in from Salvatore."

"What changes if we hear from him?" She frowned, staring into his eyes as if reaching down into his soul. "You think if that man Zhutov has blown your cover, then you don't have to make tough choices. You won't have to do the work figuring out how to let me into your life if you keep the job."

"Or maybe I'm not sure if I'll be a man worthy of you without the job." The admission hissed out between clenched teeth, something he'd known deep in his belly even if he hadn't been willing to admit it until now.

Her eyes went wide. "How in the world could you think that?"

"I'm looking reality in the face, and it sucks. You saw it all on the surveillance camera. You saw those kids in the handcuffs." The memory of it roared around inside him, echoing with flashes from his arrest, the weight of an ankle monitor, the sense of confinement that never went away no matter how freely he traveled the world. "They were stealing drugs to sell. And we could dig into why they needed the money, but bottom line is that they stole medication that's hard as hell to replace out here and they injured a guard in the process."

She gripped his arm harder, with both hands. "It had to be painful seeing the boys you'd played with betray you that way."

The sympathy in her eyes flowed over him like acid on open wounds. "Damn it, Jayne, I was one of those kids. Why can't you get that?"

"I do get it. But you changed, and there's a chance they'll change, too. Is that such a horrible thing? To believe in second chances?"

The roar inside him grew until it was all he could do to keep from shouting. She didn't deserve his rage. She didn't deserve any of this.

"I'm not the good guy you make me out to be. Yes, I took the job with Interpol to make amends, but I do the work because it gives me a high. Just like when I was in high school, like when I broke the law. I've only figured out how to channel it into something that keeps me out of jail." He looked her dead in the eyes and willed her to hear him. "I'm not the family guy you want, and I never will be."

"What if I say I'm willing to work with that? I think we can find a balance."

He would have given anything to hear those words three years ago, to have that second chance with her. But he knew better now. "And I don't. We tried, and we failed."

"Are you saying this because you're afraid I'll get hurt from something related to your job?"

Holding back a sigh, he dodged her question. He'd had plenty of practice after all. "If that was the case, I would just say it."

"Like hell. You would stage a fight to get me to walk. It's cliché, just like when I woke up with nightmares, and we're not cliché kinds of people. We lead our lives doing difficult jobs that rational people would shy away from. I love that about you, Conrad. I love you."

Damn it, why was she pushing this tonight? Did she want to end things?

And ultimately, wouldn't that be the best thing for her?

"Jayne, don't make this harder on both of us. We've been separated for three years. It's time to finalize the divorce."

Too stunned to cry, Jayne closed the bedroom door and sagged back on the thick wood panel. At least she'd made it out of that room with her head high and her eyes dry.

How in the hell was she supposed to sleep in here tonight with the memories of a few hours ago still so fresh in her mind, the scent of their lovemaking still clinging to the sheets?

Damn him for doing this to her again. And damn her for being such an idiot.

She ran to her suitcase and dug through it, tossing things onto the floor until she found the little black shoulder bag she'd worn to the casino that first night. She dug inside and pulled out her wedding ring set, the five-carat yellow diamond and matching diamond-studded band.

Her fist clenched around the pair until the stones cut into her palm. She grounded herself in the pain. It was all she could do not to run outside and throw the damn things into the river.

She squeezed her eyes closed and thought back over their fight.

Conrad meant every word he'd said. She'd seen the resolution in his eyes, heard it in his voice. And while she still believed he'd made the choice out of misconceptions about himself, she also accepted she couldn't change his mind. She couldn't force him to let go of his past.

She'd waited for him for three years. She'd come here to try one last time to get through to him, only to have him tear her heart to shreds all over again. She didn't regret trying. But she knew it would be a long time before she got over loving Conrad Hughes, if she ever did.

Now there was nothing left for her but to leave with her head high.

Putting the pieces of her life back together

would be beyond difficult and, God, she needed a shoulder to cry on, someone to share a bucket of ice cream and put life into perspective. Her mother was gone. She didn't have any sisters. Seeing Anthony again was out of the question, and her friends from work would never understand this.

The answer came to her, a place to go where Conrad couldn't argue about her safety, a person who could offer the advice, support and the sympathetic shoulder she needed. She placed her wedding rings on the bedside table, letting go of them and of Conrad for the final time. She wasn't chasing after him anymore.

She picked up her cell phone and called Hillary Donavan.

She was gone. He'd lost her for good this time.

Watching the lazy hippo roll around in the mud, Conrad sat on the dock with a bottle of Chivas, hoping to get rip-roaring drunk before the sun set. The night had been long, sitting on the couch and thinking about her in the next room. He'd prepared himself for the torment of watching over her until Salvatore cleared him to leave.

But she'd walked out first thing in the morning with her own plan in place, already cleared by Salvatore. A solid plan. As good as any he could come up with himself. Boothe would take her to the airport where Hillary would meet her.

Jayne was a smart and competent woman.

He tipped back his glass, not even tasting the fine whiskey, just welcoming the burn in his gut.

The rumble of an approaching car launched him to his feet. Then he recognized Boothe's vehicle and dropped back down to sit on the dock. He must be returning from taking Jayne to the airport.

Just what he needed. His old "friend" gloating. He topped off his drink.

Boothe's footsteps thudded down the embankment, rustling the tall grass. "You're still sitting around here feeling sorry for yourself. Damn, and I thought you were a smart guy."

Conrad glanced over his shoulder. "I don't need this crap today. Want a drink?"

"No, thanks." Boothe sat beside him, a handful of pebbles in his fist.

"Always the saint."

He pitched a pebble in the water, ripples circling outward. "People see what they want to see."

"Is there a reason you came by?"

"I've been thinking about offering your wife a job. Since you live here and own the clinic, I thought I should run the idea past you first."

Boothe surprised him again, although hadn't he had the same thought about moving Jayne to Africa and settling down? Would she actually take the position even though their paths would cross? "And you're asking my permission?"

"She's a Hospice nurse. She's already on unpaid leave from her other job because of what we do. Only seems fair to help her out." He flicked a couple more pebbles into the water. "Or did you just plan to assuage your conscience by writing her a big fat check?"

Damn, Boothe went for the jugular. "You're offering her a job to get back at me, aren't you?"

"Contrary to what you think, I don't dislike you...anymore."

"So you concede you hated my guts back then, even if you had the occasional weak moment and shared your cookies with a soulless bastard like me."

Boothe's laugh echoed out over the river, startling a couple of parrots and a flock of herons. "Hell, yes, I resented you. You were an arrogant bastard back then and you haven't learned much since."

"Remember that I write your paycheck." Conrad knocked back another swallow. "I fund your clinic."

"That's the only reason I'm here, because I'm grateful." He flung the rest of the pebbles into the water and faced him. "That woman is the best thing that's ever going to happen to you. So, because I owe you a debt, I'm going to give you a piece of advice."

"Thanks. Can I have another drink first?"

Boothe ignored him and pressed on. "In the work world, you're aggressive. You go after what you want. Why the hell haven't you gone after your wife?"

The question stunned him silent through two more rolls of his pet hippo out there.

Disgusted with himself, Conrad set aside his glass. "She wants a divorce. She's waited three years. I think that's a good sign she's serious."

"Maybe." Boothe nodded slowly. "But is that what you want? You made her come to you again and again. And if you do get back together again, she's stuck waiting for you, repeating the old pattern that wrecked her the first time."

"You're more depressing than the alcohol."

Boothe clapped him on the back, Salvatore style. "It's time for you to quit being a stupid ass. I'll even spell it out for you. Go after your wife."

"That's it?" Just show up? And he hadn't realized until now how much he'd been hoping Boothe might actually have a concrete solution, a magic fix that would bring Jayne home for good this time. Even though he'd told her to leave, the quiet afterward had been a damn hefty reminder of how empty his life was without her. He'd made a monumental mistake this time and Boothe thought that could fixed with a *hey, honey, I'm home?* "After how badly I've screwed up, that doesn't seem like nearly enough."

"For her, that's everything. Think about it." He gave him a final clap on the back before he started walking up the plateau again.

Conrad shoved to his feet, his head reeling from a hell of a lot more than booze.

"Boothe," he called out.

Rowan stopped halfway up the hill. "Yeah, brother?"

Conrad scratched along his collarbone, right over the spot that had once been broken. "Thanks for the cookie."

"No problem." The doctor waved over his shoulder.

As Boothe's car rumbled away, Conrad let his old classmate's advice roll around in his brain, lining up with memories of the past. Damn it, he'd fought for his wife. Hadn't he?

But as he looked back, he had to accept that he'd expected the marriage to fail from the start. He'd expected her to walk every bit as much as she'd expected him to follow the pattern of her old man. And when she didn't walk this time, he'd pushed her away.

Except Jayne wasn't like his parents. She couldn't be any further from his criminal of a dad or his passively crooked mother and he should have realized that. Countless times he'd accused Jayne of letting the past rule her, and he'd done the same thing. Convinced she would let him down, because, hey, he didn't deserve her anyway. So he'd pushed her away. He might not have been the one to walk out the door, but he hadn't left her any choice by rejecting her so callously. He hadn't left physically, but no question, he'd emotionally checked out on her.

She deserved better than that from him. She'd laid her heart out, something that must have been tough as hell for her after all they'd been through. He should have reassured her that she was his whole world. He worshipped the ground she walked on and his life was crap without her.

And his life would continue to be crap if he didn't get himself together and figure out how to make her believe he loved her. He'd panicked in telling her to leave. He realized now that even though he wasn't good enough for her, he would work his ass off every single day for the rest of his life to be a man worthy of her. No matter what Salvatore uncovered, regardless of whether Conrad had a career or not, he wanted to spend his life with Jayne. He trusted her with anything. Everything. He would even answer her million questions, whatever it took to make her trust him again.

To make her believe he loved her.

Twelve

The Bahamas shoreline was wasted on Jayne.

She lounged in a swimsuit and sarong on the well-protected balcony with Hillary. Most people would give anything for a vacation like this at a Nassau casino with a friend to look out for her. Her new gal pal sure knew how to nurse a broken heart in style. But for all Jayne's resolve to stand her ground, this split with Conrad hurt so much worse than the one before and she was only one day into the new breakup.

The familiar sounds drifted from the casino below and wrapped around her, echoing bells and whistles, cheers of victory and ahhhs of disappointment. Glasses clinked as the drinks flowed in the resort, while boaters and swimmers splashed in the ocean. This place had its differences from Monte Carlo, a more casual air to the high-end vacationers in sarongs and flowing sundresses, but there were still plenty of jewels around necks, in ears…and in navels.

She wasn't in much of a gambling mood. Besides, she'd left her rings behind.

What had Conrad thought as he looked at them? Did he have any regrets about pushing to finalize the divorce? How could she have been so wrong to hope he would come around this time and fight for their marriage the way he tackled every other challenge in his life?

God, she wanted to scream out her pain and frustration and she would have had she been alone. She turned to Hillary, who was stretched out on a lounger with a big floppy hat and an umbrella to protect her freckled complexion.

"Thanks for taking me in until Salvatore can clear everything up. Once he gives the go-ahead, I'll be out of your hair and back to work."

Hillary looked over the top of her sunglasses, zinc oxide on her freckled nose. "You know you never have to work again if you don't want. I don't mean to sound crass, but your divorce settlement will be quite generous."

Jayne hadn't wanted Conrad's money. She wanted the man. "I don't see myself as the dilettante type."

"Understandable, of course." Hillary twirled her straw in the fruity beverage, not looking the least like an undercover agent herself. "During my years planning events, I met many different types of people—everything from conspicuous consumers to truly devoted philanthropists. It's amazing to have the financial freedom to make a difference in such a sweeping fashion. Just something to think about."

Like opening a clinic in Africa? Conrad had definitely used his money and influence to change the world for the better. Why the hell couldn't he accept the happiness he'd earned?

The sound of the French doors opening pulled her attention back to the present.

Hillary sat up quickly, her fingers landing on the folded towel that covered a handgun. "Troy?"

A tiny canine ball of energy burst through in a frenzy of barking. Jayne gaped, stunned. Surely it couldn't be her little...

"Mimi?"

Her French bulldog raced on short legs in a black and white blur straight into her arms. Oh, my God, it *was* her dog. Mimi covered her chin in lapping kisses.

Jayne's heart tumbled over itself in her chest because there was just one way Mimi could have gotten here. Only one person who would have known how important it was to have her dog with her right now.

The final question that remained? Had Conrad delivered the dog in person as a peace offering or just arranged the travel in a final heartbreaking gesture of thoughtfulness? She squeezed her eyes shut and buried her face in Mimi's neck to hold off looking for a moment longer, to hold on to the possibility that her husband might be standing behind her even now.

Bracing herself, she looked back and found, thank God, Conrad stood in the open doorway. Her heart leaped into her throat and her eyes feasted on the sight of him after a nightmarish day of thinking she would never see him again. He wore jeans, a button-down shirt with rolled-up sleeves—and dark circles under his haunted eyes.

She didn't rejoice in the fact that he'd been miserable, too—okay, maybe she did a little—but above all she wanted him to be happy. He deserved to be happy. They both did.

A rustling sounded from the lounger beside her as Hillary stood. "Is there word on Zhutov?"

Jayne sat upright, swinging her legs to the side of her own lounger. Why hadn't she considered he might be here for that reason? If Zhutov had broken Conrad's cover, ending his career with Interpol, then she would never know if he would have returned to her on his own. Trust would be all the tougher when they already had so much between them.

Bottom line, she wanted what was best for

him, his cover safe, even if that meant he walked away from her.

Conrad shook his head. "No word on Zhutov yet. I'm here for Jayne. Just Jayne."

He stared straight into her eyes as he spoke, his voice deep and sure. She almost forgot to breathe. And while she was disappointed not to have Salvatore give them the all clear, she couldn't help but be grateful that whatever Conrad had to say wasn't motivated by losing his work with Interpol.

Hillary grabbed her bag and her hat. "I'll, uh, just step into the kitchen and make, um… Hell. I'll just leave." Her hand fell on Jayne's shoulder lightly. "Call if you need me."

Angling sideways past Conrad, Hillary slipped away into the suite, closing the door behind her.

Jayne hugged her dog closer as Mimi settled into her lap. "This was thoughtful of you. How did you get her here?"

He stuffed his hands in his pockets and eyed her warily. "I phoned your friend Anthony and asked for help retrieving the dog."

"You spoke to him?"

Conrad nodded, pushing away from the door and stepping closer. "I did. He's a nice guy actually, and he was glad to pick up Mimi and take her to the airport because he knew seeing her would make you smile." He crouched beside her, one knee on the ground. "Which I have to tell you, makes me feel like a mighty small bastard, because I should have thought to do this sooner. I should have thought to do and say a lot of things. But I'm here to make that right."

The hope she'd restrained in her heart swelled as she heard him out, her thoughtful husband who knew she would appreciate her precious dog far more than a lifeless diamond bracelet. "I'm listening."

"I'm sorry for telling you we should make the divorce final. I was certain I would let you down again, so I acted like an idiot." He drew in a shaky breath as if…nervous. The great Conrad Hughes, Wall Street Wizard and casino magnate was actually anxious. "I'm a numbers man, always have been, ever since I was a kid counting out my French fries into equal piles. I'm not good at seeing the middle ground in a situation. But I'm getting there."

"What do you propose?" she asked and saw no hesitation in his eyes as he opened up and answered her.

"Compromise." He met her gaze full-on, such sincerity in his espresso dark eyes they steamed with conviction. "On *my* part this time. When we were together before I asked you to do all the changing and insulted you by giving nothing in return."

And clearly that was tearing him apart now.

"Not nothing. You're being too tough on yourself. You always are." She sketched her fingers along his unshaven jaw. Apparently he hadn't wasted a second getting to her, between arranging to pick up Mimi and flying to the Bahamas. He hadn't even stolen a second to shave.

"Then you'll help me work through that." He pressed a kiss into her palm. "Jayne, I've faced down criminals. Made and given away fortunes. But the thought of losing you nearly drives me

to my knees. I see you with all that uncondi-
tional love in your eyes, a total openness I never
gave back. You knew the truth about me and my
crooked family, and you loved me anyway. I'd
put us in an all-or-nothing life. Well, the past
three years of 'nothing' has been hell."

"I completely agree with you there." Her eyes
burned, but with happy tears and hope.

"But back to my compromise. And if it's not
good enough, tell me and I promise you, I will
listen to you this time. After you left, I realized
I can't go through this again. I let you go once,
and it almost killed me."

"Conrad? I don't know what to say." How funny
that *she* was the one speechless now. She'd hoped
for a moment like this, prayed that Conrad could
find the peace to embrace a life together, but the
reality of it sent joy sparkling through her.

"If you want me to quit the Interpol work, I
will."

"Shh!" She touched her fingertips to his
mouth, moved that he would offer, hopeful that
he truly was willing this time to make the com-

promises needed to build a life together. "You don't have to do that. I just need reassurances that you're all right."

He nipped her fingers lightly, smiling his appreciation. "I can do that. I will tell you everything I'm cleared to share about my work with Salvatore. I can promise you I'll check in every twenty-four hours so you won't worry."

"And that's safe for you?"

"We have the best of the best technology. And I intend to make use of it to keep you reassured—and to keep you well protected. I kept pushing you away to keep you safe, but all it did was tear us both apart. I will do better. And if you change your mind about the job with Interpol, say the word, I'm out. I would give up anything to keep you. I honest to God love you that much, Jayne."

Unable to hold back any longer, she leaned forward into his arms and kissed him, pouring all the love, hope and dreams out and feeling them flow right back to her, from him. There was something different in him now; the restlessness was gone. And while it had shredded her heart to walk away from him again, maybe that's what it had taken to make him see what she'd already realized—they needed each other. Two pieces of the same whole. Conrad seemed to understand that now. He'd found a new peace and maybe even some forgiveness for himself.

Mimi squirmed to get free, squished between them. Laughing, they eased apart and her dog—their dog—jumped from Jayne's lap to sniff the balcony furniture and potted plants.

Jayne looked back at Conrad, still kneeling in front of her. "Is it all right to have a dog here?"

"I bought the place two years ago. I can have a whole damn pack of dogs inside if I want."

"And is that what you want? A pack?" She toyed with the open V of his collar, the fire rekindling inside her.

"Actually I was thinking more like a soccer team of kids. Our kids, babies first, of course."

Shock froze her. She stared into his eyes and found one hundred percent sincerity.

"I'd like that, too," she whispered.

She'd learned to leave the past behind and step outside her safety zone without losing the essence of herself. Life wasn't an all-or-nothing game. It was a blending of the best of both sides. A marriage.

Her marriage.

Just as she started to reach for her husband, the French doors opened and Hillary stuck her head out, cell phone in hand. "Folks, you're going to want to hear this update from Salvatore."

Jayne's stomach knotted. Was it bad news? Could their newfound peace be so short-lived? She felt Conrad take her hand and squeeze reassuringly. She looked into his eyes and realized she wasn't alone—and neither was he. They truly were a team now and whatever happened, they would face it together.

She turned back to Hillary, and realized the woman was smiling so brightly the news couldn't be that bad.

Conrad said, "We're ready. What's the update?"

Hillary tapped speakerphone and Salvatore's voice rumbled over the airwaves, "Authorities apprehended Zhutov's hired assassin and given his confession and the photos he had on his cell phone, we're certain you two were not the targets. You're in the clear. Your cover is secure."

Grinning, Conrad grabbed Jayne around the waist, lifted her from the chair and spun her around. Mimi barked, dancing around their feet. Laughing, Hillary put the phone to her ear and stepped back into the hotel suite.

Jayne grasped Conrad's shoulders as he lowered her back to the ground again. "Oh, my God, that is amazing news."

"Damn straight it is." He hauled her to his chest, a sigh of relief rattling through him. "And Lord willing, the day's about to get even better."

Stepping back again, he pulled his hand out of his pocket, their wedding rings rested in his palm. "Jayne, I've loved you from the first time I saw you and will love you until I draw my last breath. Will you please do me the honor of wearing this ring?"

She placed her hand over his, their rings together in their clasped hands. "I'm all in. I want to be a part of your big, bold plans for the future, to help others in the clinic in Africa and build more clinics in other parts of the world. I accept you, as you are... I *love* you as you are."

His hand slid into her hair, and he guided her mouth to his with a fierce tenderness that reached all the way to her soul.

The stakes had been high, but she knew a winning hand when she saw one.

Smoothly, Conrad slid on his wedding band and then he slipped hers back on her finger. Where it would stay put this time.

Because one pair, the two of them, had won it all.

Epilogue

Two months later

Coming home to his wife was one of life's greatest pleasures.

Conrad parked the Land Cruiser beside the clinic where his wife worked. Their clinic, in Africa. He'd offered Jayne diamonds and a splashy jet-set lifestyle, but his wife had chosen a starkly majestic home in Africa, caring for the ill and orphaned in the area villages.

God, he loved her and her big, caring heart.

His eyes were drawn to her like a magnet to the purest, strongest steel. He found her on the playground with the kids, kicking the soccer ball, her hair flying around her.

She'd stepped in to help run the foundation that oversaw the clinic. In the two months since she'd relocated here, she'd already come up with plans and funding to add an official childcare center so when adults came for treatment they didn't have to bring their kids inside where they could catch anything from pneumonia to a simple cold.

He'd tried to tell her she didn't have to work this hard, but she'd only rolled her eyes and told him they could sneak away for an opera once a month—if he promised to be incredibly naughty before intermission. In spite of his efforts to pamper her, he'd discovered his wife had grown fiercely independent. The way she took charge, her visionary perspective, reminded him of Colonel Salvatore.

Zhutov was no longer even a remote threat. One morning a month ago, guards had found him dead in his bunk, smothered. Most likely by someone as payback for any one of his criminal acts over the years.

Life was balancing out.

Conrad started toward the soccer field. Now that the loose ends had been tied up this past week he'd spent at Interpol Headquarters in Lyon, France, he was free until the next assignment rolled around.

He liked coming home to her, here. He could manage his holdings from a distance with good managers in place, and he could jet over with his wife whenever she was ready to take in an opera.

Right now, though, he just wanted to have dinner with his wife. The soccer ball came flying in his direction, and he booted it back into play. Jayne waved, smiling as she jogged toward him.

"Welcome home," she called, throwing her arms around his neck.

He caught her, spinning her around under the warm African sun. Already, she whispered about her plans for making love in the shower before supper and how good it would be to sleep next to him again.

And he had to agree, his insomnia was now a thing of the past. Everything was better with her in his life. He knew, in his wife's arms, he'd finally come home.

* * * * *